This fictional story's origin is purely that of the writer's imagination. Therefore, any characters, themes, and/or plots are entirely coincidental. And should be regarded as such.

Warning –

The content of these novels is for pure entertainment and superfluous education. No item, herb, spell, or ritual in these books should be performed or ingested by anyone without the proper cleansing, overstanding, or supervision. Remember, all true wisdom comes from within and flows without. As above, so below; as within, so without.

Also, By Luna Charles

Men Are Not the Problem

- Vol I, II & III

My Life, My Rules

- Vol I & II

The Door – Short

The Healer's Persecution – Short

The Choices Made – Short

In the Beginning – Short

- Part of the Lilith Series

Daughters' Of Lilith - Good Food – BK 1

MAKTUB Trist Group

Presents

Good Food

An Understanding Of Basic Alchemy

The Daughters of Lilith Series
Book 2

Luna Charles

Table of Contents

Chapter XIX - *Fennel* 8

Chapter XX- *Cleavers* 18

Chapter XXI- *Cinnamon* 27

Chapter XXII -Cardamom 39

Chapter XXIII-*Spikenard* 49

Chapter XXIV- *Mint* 58

Chapter XXV- *Lavender* 68

Chapter XXVI - *Hemp* 76

Chapter XXVII - *Garlic* 85

Chapter XXVIII -*Paprika* 99

Chapter XXIX – Bluebells 108

Chapter XXX - Mallow...122

Chapter XXXI - Spanish Needle 138

Chapter XXXII – *Coriander* 146

Chapter XXXIII – *Mugwort* 158

Chapter XXXIV - *Licorice Root* 167

Chapter XXXV – *Sorrel* 179

For seekers of the truth

The secrets of alchemy exist to transform mortals from a state of suffering and ignorance to a state of enlightenment and bliss.

-   **Deepak Chopra**

Chapter XIX - *Fennel*

Fennel is a flowering plant species in the carrot family. It is a hardy, perennial herb with yellow flowers and feathery leaves indigenous to the Mediterranean's shores. Fennel seeds have antioxidant, anti-inflammatory, anti-fungal, and antiviral effects.

In Spiritual Work – to use for *all-around defense, plant fennel around your house. Fennel seeds can be placed close to windows to ward off evil spirits and unwelcome guests.*

In 1791, Ceres stood at the ritual site that would become the founding moment of the Haitian Revolution. Dutty Boukman was speaking with the force of someone who had caught the holy Spirit at Sunday service — the kind that made the whole congregation catch it with him.

"*Om baba kaliba sata omwe,*" He repeated.

One of the men carrying the pot came up from behind with a ladle in hand. Boukman continued to speak as he lowered the bowl and let the liquid from the cauldron be poured into the bowl of blood. Boukman swirled the container around for a moment. Then, he refilled the ladle from the mixture in the bowl and ran it back into the pot. As this happened, three new men came from the direction they had taken here.

"*Erzulie,*" He called loudly over the crowd.

"*Greata Spiri' come to wi, make wi strong as ya mountains, carry wi to victory as wi fight da enemy. Let wi blood oath an' wi sacred promise be the payment to ya. Give wi strengt,' make wi weapon to cut threw wi enemies like wi cuts dem sugarcanes. Lead wi, mighty Erzulie, wi fallow. Give wi men, woman, chil' powa ova wi enemi.*"

The three stood shoulder-to-shoulder, a mere three feet from Boukman and Cécile, The High Priest and Priestess that carried out the freedom ritual, blocking Ceres' view. As she moved to see past them, Ceres noticed one of the men's eyes seemed to follow her movement as Boukman had done earlier. However, he was shorter and thinner than the others, and his face was dark and scarred.

"Jean-François Papillon," Boukman called loudly over the madding crowd, pulling the thin man's attention from Ceres.

One of the other men stepped forward. He was wearing dark blue long pants and a long-sleeved white shirt. He was a tall man with skin as dark as the sky and a state regality about him that made Ceres doubt that he was a slave. Jean-François Papillon looked into Boukman's eyes and bowed his head down slightly.

"Do ya swear to wi Gods dat ya denounce they God? dat ya sha'll fo'ever praise wi Gods? dat ya shall go into the night wit faith wi Gods protec' ya?" Boukman continued.

"I do," Jean-François Papillon replied.

Handing him the bowl, Jean-François Papillon drank from the concoction. The Priest returned the container and moved to the second man down the line.

"Georges Biassou," he called out over the crowd. A shorter man moved forward with the stride of an ex-military man. *"Do ya swear to wi Gods dat ya denounce they God? dat ya sha'll*

fo'ever praise wi Gods? Dat ya shall go into the night wit faith wi Gods protec' ya?"

"*I do,*" acknowledged Georges Biassou as he repeated the ritual, drank from the same bowl, and returned it to Boukman. The drums seemed to be getting louder, and the air was electrified.

Finally, Boukman called out Jeannot over the crowd.

The man who had seemingly been able to see Ceres stepped forward. He looked from Ceres to Cecile to Boukman with sharp, piercing black eyes and dark brown lips. And even though he was smaller and thinner than the other men, he made Ceres feel like he was the destroyer of worlds.

"*Do ya swear to wi Gods dat ya denounce they God? dat ya sha'll fo'ever praise wi Gods? Dat ya shall go into the night wit faith wi Gods protec' ya?*"

"*I do,*" the more petite man agreed.

From eastward, the wind howled like a wolf calling to its pack. A once clear sky filled with pregnant clouds as the drumbeats grew to the level of cacophony.

Cécile picked up her chant again.

"*Erzulie manman, Kote ou yey.*" Other women in the crowd joined her.

"*Tis God who made da sun, who brin's wi light from above, who raises da sea, an' who makes da storm rumble. Dat God is there, do ya understand? He watches wi, hiding in a cloud, watches his grandchil're, and sees all da whites do! Da God of da whites pushes 'em to crime, but he wants wi to do good deeds. But da God who is so good orders wi to vengeance. He will direct wi hands and give wi help. Thro' away da image of da God of da whites who thirsts fa wi tears. Listen dat liberty dat speaks in all wi hearts."*

As Boukman spoke, the crowd stomped in unison with the drums. Torches had been lit and passed from hand to hand through the mass of people.

"Tonight, is da night of da people whose blood has soak'd da Eart of tis country," Cécile shouted. Ceres swore she saw gossamer silver wings spreading outward from her back as she spoke.

"Tonight, wi tak back wi freedom, wi pride, wi strength!"

The crowd exploded into a thunderous roar simultaneously. Then, the sky burst open, and a monsoon of water fell from the sky. Again, the crowd screamed louder, and the wind, not to be outdone, grew more assertive.

How can the plantation owners not hear this? Ceres thought.

Suddenly, a large black boar came rushing from the clearing. Both Boukman and Cécile stopped speaking to look at it. It stood motionless, looking at them, its white tusk glistening in the light as it snorted loudly into the air.

"Erzulie will lead da way!" Boukman screamed and moved toward the boar.

The animal, in turn, let out a loud grunt and ran straight towards the Priest and Priestess, splashing reddish water in its wake, dodging around the pair, and passing the fiery pot. Then, it headed west toward the flickering candle and fire lights that Ceres had not seen before but guessed it was the plantations.

"The time is now!!" Boukman shouted and chased after the boar, followed by the three ordained men, Cécile, and the crowd.

Ceres was pulled forward into the action like a swimmer caught in a riptide.

How far will this dream take me?

The rain was torrential. The ground had turned into muddy copper under their feet. Ceres could feel the slimy mud in between her toes as she ran. The leaves brushed against her cheeks harshly as the crowd's momentum carried her forward. Her breath fell short. As she moved with them, the motion was almost surreal. The drums were still beating in the background. Then, a young woman running with a torch passed her in full battle cry and fury, her eyes locked ahead, neither looking left nor right. *She thought this is how freedom is won, with no hesitation and a clear focus.* The air in her lungs was heating up with every step, and her footsteps thundered in her ears. She kept running full-on with no fear of where her next move might land.

Then darkness took hold of her.

Ceres coughed, choking out a breath as she sat suddenly on the beach house couch. Her mother, Diana, eyes glazed over, was still at her feet, and her sister, Magalie, was slumped forward in the chair, her head resting on the back of the couch. The young Priestess went to stand, but a figure moved into her peripherals. The woman seemed surreal, only the essence of a being made of gossamer threads. She kneeled before the young woman, whose consciousness was only partially on this plane, and kissed her gently on the forehead.

Ceres fell back into the Dream-cast on the couch and the loving caress of a tunnel of light.

The three phantom women picked up their chanting anew.

Ceres awoke in a room lit by a large fire across from a small man on the other side of the vortex. He wore black breeches that stopped at the knee with a center front opening. The legs gathered into a band above the knee, closing with white ties in a white shirt with lace down the front of it, and the end of his sleeves was mainly open, with sweat sliding down his bare chest. Minor stains of blood splattered the bottom of the shirt. She couldn't tell how tall he was standing there with curly black hair tied in a ponytail and a face so pale that he did not look like he had ever seen sunlight.

He was screaming at her,

"Tu stupide, incompétent, nègre!"

A glass of wine in his hand splattered on the wooden floor. Ceres tried to understand what he was saying, but her mind was still too scattered to parse the French around her confusion.

As her mind cleared, she realized she was in a large room. The walls were tightly packed with square white bricks, reflecting the light from the large stone fireplace the stranger was in front of. A painting above the mantle showed what could have been the man screaming at her and a beautiful woman with blonde hair and blue eyes, wearing a red bodice dress with white lace draping down the front and a green petticoat that matched his trousers. To the side of the fire was a wooden table and two high-back chairs in green-and-gold baroque. An almost empty container of red wine sat on the table.

Ceres thought she heard music and laughter coming from somewhere nearby. *There must be a party*, she thought. She turned toward the sounds and saw a door with light coming from underneath it, not far from where she stood. At the same time, Ceres' knee hit something painfully. She winced and looked down, seeing she was standing in front of a bench. It was also in the same green-and-gold baroque design as the chairs, with curved arms and padded seats. And behind the ottoman was a four-poster bed draped with white-and-green lace curtains. The bed sent a shock wave of fear through Ceres.

She moved toward the door, but a sudden sound of glass shattering to the floor made her turn toward the angry man, just in time for him to slap her across the face. The hit was so intense that she fell to her knees in pain, holding onto the nearby bench.

"Where the fuck do you think you're going?" He was still speaking French, but now Ceres could understand him.

Grabbing her by her wool-like hair, he yanked her forward onto the floor. With a grunt, he fell on top of her. He slapped her again as he tore at the top of her white dress. His green eyes were inflamed with rage. She screamed, trying to push him off of her, but she was small. She tasted blood when he hit next. The stench from the wine on his breath made her want to vomit. Instead, she screamed again, louder this time. Undoubtedly, someone heard her.

Nevertheless, no one came. Ceres opened her mouth once more. This time, the hit made her blackout.

She came with him, looking down at her on the floor as he fixed his clothes.

"Get your lazy ass up and clean this mess up," he told her.

She tried to move, but her whole body was in pain, so much agony from everywhere. She started crying as she sat up slowly. The throbbing coming from between her legs made her groan. He kicked her in the side.

"Hurry, my wife might come in at any time now, and I don't want her to know I wasted what might be our heir on a slave girl." He tossed his bloodied, sweaty shirt at her face.

"Tell the old woman to make sure she does a good job cleaning this, or it will cost you a night's meal."

Chapter XX- *Cleavers*

Cleavers enhance the lymphatic system's function and improve its ability to flush out toxins, decrease congestion, and reduce swelling. The lymph-cleansing action of this herb, in turn, enhances the immune system's function.

In Spiritual Work: *Cleavers are commonly used in binding spells and matters of commitment. Use in spells or mojo bags that deal with commitment issues, rocky relationships, and love.*

Ahkter and Mahkter, the Albino Jesuit twins, waited almost a lifetime to retrieve the second Book of Knowledge, with its Reader securely bonded to it, only for the second Book to fail to reveal anything. Angrily, the brothers broke a promise to Jean and sought his son out for a sample of his blood. At least with Mateo's blood, they could read a page or two in the first year, as they did with the Ashanti Book. But, unfortunately, acquiring the elusive Mateo Dieudonne's blood took another year, and even with the blood, The Book revealed nothing. The Sons' disappointment was still raw in the memory of the twins, who had been charged with the task.

In retrospect, the brothers believe the bonding spell had worked precisely as it was supposed to. They knew what they had received from the first Book had been an instrument of protection against people like The Sons of Eve, who believed the world was meant to be Patriarchal. It bonded the next Book of Knowledge so no one could read it. Not even with its current Reader's lineage's blood. Therefore, ultimately cutting the line of information that would have revealed the following Book's location.

Yet, tonight, they were attempting to get a reaction from the second Book by dripping Mateo's blood on yet another section. The Book flipped closed in Mahkter's hand, glowing in white light. Causing Ahkter, who was standing beside his brother, to take a step back. Just before, an ethereal image of a tall, dark woman wearing thin white fabric, with the bottom of her face veiled, appeared in The Book. The image towered over them for a few seconds. Looked around as if it was confused about its surroundings. It spoke without speaking, her words echoing in their head,

"*Les étoiles se sont alignées*," then vanished.

The profound event had left the brothers aghast.

They were not used to that kind of power activating without the proper rituals being put into action. Furthermore, the type of power they were attempting to understand lay entirely outside the knowledge of The Sons. A divine insight that seemed to flow through the African blood. But new to The Order of The Sons of Eve Paradigm because they never thought it important enough to learn about it. Even though they had actively suppressed it.

The Africans and their lineage's knowledge of how to work with the Divine Spirit were older than some would want to believe. African spiritualism predated the Luciferian magic, which most pagan practices were known to use.

Looking at the door, the twins were heading towards it with the protective sigils reinforced with a spell carved into it. Ahkter wondered if the sigils on that door could protect them from such knowledge.

Pulling the ornamented metal door handles open in unison as their fingerprints automatically released the lock. The two men walked into the large, circular-shaped, multi-level room. The library was a self-contained, one-of-a-kind repository of sacred knowledge. Each item inside was a scroll, a tablet, a manuscript, or a tome, held in individual airtight glass containers, accessible only by authorized thumbprints. The Library was currently empty, as it was almost always. Its location was one of the great secrets of The Sons, with very few people having the privilege of accessing it and even fewer being able to access it anytime they wanted.

In the center of the room sat a polygon-shaped table with seating for 12. The 12 seats were occupied, and no one entered. Those seats and the 12 names they belong to were among The Sons' most coveted secrets. Their names had never been known to more than four people throughout history. Now, in an age when most information is digitized for faster access to their different sectors. At the same time, threats from well-funded conspiracy theorists' hackers with Liberal deep pockets had made it necessary to reduce the number of members that knew those twelve names from four to two.

After the image vanished, the brothers regained some form of composure. Mahkter noticed the striped diamond on the cover of the Book, and the six stars around it were now glowing.

The brother's mind went into overdrive, trying to figure out what celestial event the image could have been speaking about when the phantom woman in white appeared over the Book and said, '*The stars are aligned.*' They quickly deduced that anything star-related had to do with the celestial bodies and had come straight to the library to look at the heavenly maps of astronomers from long ago. Specifically, those that would have been done by the Moorish travelers were once held in The Library of Alexandria.

The library was organized into sections. Each section was a cluster of the knowledge they had acquired from that group. They have everything of importance that ever existed, whether it was the Old Gods of the North, The Grecian, or the Roman Pantheon. The Spirits of the Native Americans and South Americans. The Hebrew Kabbalah, Hinduism mysticism, and The Books of Christianity held out of the Bible, but unfortunately, a minimal amount of acquired knowledge regarding the Spiritual practices of one of the largest continents on earth, Africa.

They were looking for the writings of one specific Astronomer, Philosopher, and Theologian who traveled through West Africa before the slave trades, Abū Ishāq Ibrāhīm al-Zarqālī: more specifically, his paper on the *"Tables of Toledo,"* An Almanac of Celestial events. The brothers knew that things were happening cosmically that changed the energy flow here on Earth. Most people do not pay attention to those things, forgetting that human beings are creations, like the sun that feeds us. We all work together, everything in its place.

The one-of-a-kind 'Tables of Toledo' they were looking for were hand-drawn by Abū Ishāq, a mathematician, astronomer, and astrological instrument maker. The chart had been left for safekeeping in a Mosque, which was subsequently raided by the Templars. Since then, it has only been seen by a few dozen people throughout history. The paper came to this Library once The Order of the Sons of Eve had been created.

Bringing all the leaders of the Abrahamic teachings together under one goal.

The twins were particularly interested in seeing if any writings mentioned the forbidden knowledge of the Orishas during the time of the Moorish Empire. And if there were mentions of a Tetrad of Lunar eclipses, which was presently happening. The Brothers had proposed this theory to The Order, but the majority believed it to be of no consequence since the previous series of Tetrad Lunar Eclipses was uneventful. Nonetheless, the two men trusted their keen sense of things. And felt a swelling undercurrent of energy that seems to have passed through the minority populous.

They had been obtuse for not paying more attention to the hidden powers that lay dormant in the people of that dark continent. But, as the Americans say, they had 'missed the forest for the trees. Dismissing the few but historical flashes of insurmountable power shown to be able to be harnessed by their women's Spiritual leaders as random rather than eventful. Even though those flashes had caused ripples across time and space.

Ahkter used the one-person hydraulic lift to reach the room's second floor. He had repositioned it to the right using the carefully laid-out rails until he had reached the section where the container with the drawing was. Pressing his thumb to the circular glass reader, the glass case clicked once and slid out of its place on the shelf. The older of the twins, the container in hand, began to descend back down to his brother.

The twins walked with the container to one of the six two-person desks around the room. No one but the 12 was allowed to sit at the polygon table at any time, for any reason. Ahkter sat with the case, flipping the container's cover to retrieve the large book. Abū Ishāq Ibrāhīm al-Zarqālī was not the only astronomer to be part of organizing this detailed documentation of the night skies and its celestial events, past, and future.

The brothers knew The Book's currently trapped Reader's heritage could be traced to that part of the world. Therefore, they believed his writing would be a great place to start.

The writings the brothers were looking at were in their original Arabic form. However, Abū Ishāq had written most of the scroll while living in Spain under Spanish skies. The scrolls featured columns of notations in red and black ink against yellowing paper, some of the handwriting smeared and would have been eligible to most. But since the brothers were found, adopted, and raised by The Brotherhood over the last 50 years. The twin had learned to read, write, and decipher the hardest-to-read text in various languages, such as Latin, French, Arabic, Aramaic, Spaniard, German, and Celt. They were still hard-pressed to learn dialects from the lower part of the African continent. The Order took it as a personal insult. They had not seen nor felt the built-up of energy growing from the people of that continent. Whom the slave traders had scattered worldwide.

Ahkter was 50 pages into the manuscript, skinning each line by hovering over it with the tip of his finger, looking for any dates or annotations that would mean something. When Mahkter pointed at something stopping him where he was. The brothers looked at the annotation in mute silence. They had hoped they would find something, but now that the twins had, they were unsure what to do with it.

The notation read.

28/09/15 - stars align - debt paid.

Mahkter looked at his older brother solemnly,

"Dear God, that's in two days. We must break the oath to him; we need access to the next Reader. We need his niece, Philia."

Ahkter rubbed his trimmed white beard thoughtfully before he replied,

"We can use a locator spell with his blood we still have. I'm sure his niece will be close to him."

Chapter XXI- *Cinnamon*

Cinnamon is one of the most beneficial spices on Earth, which has antioxidant, anti-inflammatory, anti-diabetic, anti-microbial, immunity-boosting, and potential cancer, and heart disease-protecting abilities. In addition, it helps defend the brain against developing neurological disorders such as Parkinson's and Alzheimer's.

Spiritual Work: *It is used to gain wealth and success. Before a big meeting, mix a dash of cinnamon into hand lotion. Moisturize your hands while visualizing a successful outcome in your favor. Shake every decision-maker's hand that is present.*

"Yes, Monsieur Attiman," she heard herself answer in someone else's voice. A young girl's voice.

The man who had just raped her unlocked the door and walked into a lighted hall, chiming with laughter and merriment. Ceres' spirit was seething inside the girl on the floor, crying into the bloody shirt. Then, she slowly got up, moved toward the broken glass on the floor, and started picking up the pieces.

Ceres wanted to rip him apart. She felt as if she would become unglued by what had just happened. The physical pain of the experience was unbearable. This was not like the ceremony...; this abuse had been actual.

She felt all her pain, fear, and hope that someone would walk in. She sensed all of it, and she hated him for it. The girl gathered all the shirt pieces and held them close to cover the ripped parts of her dress top. She took a deep, measured breath, gathered herself up, and began to walk toward the door. On her way, she paused as she saw a mirror and stopped for a moment to look at herself. The girl was no older than thirteen, small, and thin. She had a clear brown complexion, curly black hair, a small round nose, and slanted clear brown eyes. The young girl's eyes and pink lips would have been beautiful if not marred with bruises and drying blood.

Ceres guessed by the clothes and decor she was still in the eighteenth century, but where she wasn't sure. Then, shaking still and quietly sobbing, she walked out the door and instantly found herself in the kitchen. Ceres realized that although this Dreamcast's sensory experience differed, its movement's fluidity remained exact, continuous, and shifting like a lucid dream, one moment melting into another.

She walked into a room with large, grey stone floors packed tightly with mortar, still hearing the music from a distance. Across was an eight-foot-tall heath with copper pans and ladles hanging on iron nails off the walls. A fire roared with large copper pots hanging over it on a black metal bar. Spices and herbs were drying on different hooks around the room, and a large wooden bench table with two large wooden benches on either side. On top of the table were a few large, brown-spotted birds with blue head feathers waiting to be plucked, oils in glass containers, spices, pies still steaming, and different pieces of bread ready to serve in woven baskets. It would have smelled wonderful if it were not for her pain.

A large woman was hovering over open-fired pots, her back to the kitchen entrance. She turned quicker than you would have anticipated for a woman that size and came face-to-face with the disheveled young girl. It took only a second to read the girl's state. The young girl dropped to her knees with a low wail, and the older woman rushed to her side — dreadlocks swinging, tears already on her chiseled face — and pulled the small frame into a tight embrace.

"My Astar, my Astar," she cried, holding on to the small girl's frame with such strength, yet still so gentle it did not hurt her.

Astar just stood there, gripping the shirt stained with her blood. She held it like it was a talisman, crying. She had no words, and Ceres' Spirit inside her screamed in anger, but there was no recourse.

"Madana," Astar said softly through tears.

"Mr. Attiman needs his shirt cleaned and the blood removed." Her body shook and convulsed with her words. Madana let go of her and retrieved a nearby chair.

"Come, child," Madana said, taking the bundle from Astar's arms. Then, sitting the young girl on the chair, she wiped her face with an apron. There were still tears running down Madana's face. Her jaw now clenched into a hardened resolve.

"Do you remember your mother?"

"Yes," Astar replied with a deep heave.

"Yes," she repeated, quieter this time.

"Tell me about her."

"She was beautiful, tall, and strong, wise too, like all Oromo people from the land of Cush." She paused.

"Our people's story says we are wise because we are the great-great-grandchildren of the first woman. We are strong because our blood is strong and connects directly to Earth and to Father God. I am not Oromo. I am neither wise nor strong."

Astar stayed silent for a moment. Only the movement of her shoulders and tears rolling down her face illustrated her inner pain. Then, pulling the girl close, Madana held her there with tears running down her face.

Ceres could feel the turmoil in her heart and mind; the blood in her veins was boiling, and her hands were shaking. She wished she could comfort the small child through the centuries of separation. She wanted to avenge her. She wanted so many things, yet Ceres was only a ghost. A spectator seeing a performance in which she could not interfere.

A loud whooshing sound caused Ceres to lose her breath, sending her gasping for air. Then, the world around her went dark.

"It's okay, Cherie, it's okay. It's not real, Ceres. Come back to us," She heard a voice say to her in the distance.

The whooshing had stopped, but the darkness had not abated. Ceres felt heavy. Her head was swimming and queasy, like when she and Dax drank too much at Dax's graduation party. Ceres often thought about Dax. She had been a good friend in high school who got Ceres out of her shell. But passed away from cystic fibrosis a year ago.

Ceres heard screaming and crying and thought more about Astar. How small she was, how young. Ceres' mind raced. Her thoughts merged and folded upon themselves. The colors swirled, and she caught her breath. She repeatedly blinked to clear her vision as she saw five women looking down at her. She blinked more, and the five turned to two, her mother and sister.

No, there were five, Ceres corrected herself.

The other three seemed to be made of sunlight and ethereal phantoms of ether. Ceres' body shook with every scream she thought she heard from the child. Soon, Ceres realized it was herself. She heard cries of pain she had carried with her from the past.

Ceres suddenly sat up straight with her eyes wide open.

****

Diana, who was at her feet, looked directly into her daughter's eyes. They were empty, pupils fully dilated. She slumped back onto the couch. Diana got up and sat next to where her daughter lay. Ceres' face contoured, and her eyes moved behind her closed lids as though she was having a violent dream.

"Magalie, in the box, there is a bottle with a green liquid in it. Hand it to me, please," Diana requested, pointing toward the wooden box underneath the coffee table.

Magalie moved the box to the top of the table and opened it. After rummaging through several bottles that contained green liquid, she found the correct one.

"Uncork it and hand it to me," Their mother instructed.

Magalie did as she was told. Her olfactory sense was filled with the scent of peppermint. With a questioning look, she handed the bottle to her mother. Then, reading her daughter's expression, Diana explained.

"Peppermint will wash out whatever is left of the tea in her system and help her sleep. It's mixed with rosemary and lavender tincture for healing and a night of calmer sleep."

Ceres took the drink down easier than her mother had expected her to. Within a few minutes, her demeanor changed, and she was calmly asleep. Diana sat there for a while, holding her eldest's hand, her eyebrows furrowed with worry. Had she done it right? Diana had no one to ask. Her mother was dead, and Diana didn't remember how she reacted to the Dreamcast, so she had no apparent reference. Still, her Spirit told her this was not the Dreamcast. This had something to do with Ceres herself.

Magalie sat on the coffee table, close enough to her sister and mother to touch them with her knees. She took one of Ceres' hands into one of hers and one of her mother's hands into the other. Diana took Ceres' free hand and closed the circle. Quietly, they sat there momentarily, the two Bastille women who were awake drawing strength from one another, each silently feeding power to the third.

Then softly, almost unperceivable, Magalie started reciting one of the few things that had brought her comfort as a child when she was scared and didn't understand what she was seeing. Diana, hearing her daughter's words on the wind, joined in.

> "... hallowed be thy Name,
> Thy kingdom come,
> Thy will be done,
> On earth, as it is in Heaven.
> Give us this day our daily bread.
> And forgive us our trespasses,
> As we forgive those
> Who trespasses against us?
> And lead us not into temptation,

But deliver us from evil.
For thine is the kingdom
and the power, and the glory,
Forever and ever. Amen."

Leaving them to their comforting prayers, the three ancestors returned to their points of view in their realm. Ceres would wake up thrice during the journey before finally seeing the sunrise over the horizon. She felt something standing next to her the first time she was awakened. There was an unknown, unidentifiable pressure in the air, which made her wary. She opened her eyes hesitantly, moving her head in a way she hoped was imperceptible to whoever might have been around her, only to find her winged friend standing next to her. Its silver-like wings had a pinkish tint to them now as he stood looking down at her, his eyes gazing over her softly, inquiring.

'*We have gone far*, he said, '*further, still, we have to go*,' He spoke while walking around the room.

****

Confusion gave way to relief. Ceres turned to him and asked,

"What part of me are you, and where do we have to go?"

The apparition's features softened further. Ceres felt the expression of love and empathy on his face for her, like a loving husband attempting to comfort his scared wife.

'I am you, the eternal you. The Spirit within the body that connects you to the All,'

"My soul is male," Ceres scoffed skeptically.

'Am I your soul?' He seemed to ponder this momentarily, *'Some people refer to us like that. Some refer to us as Spirit Guides, Spirit Companions, or Familiar Spirit, but none are right. The language of the tongue is lacking when trying to properly explain the mechanics of the Eternal world. I can try to explain, but the words will only leave you with a vague understanding,'*

'Your conscious mind,' he continued as he walked to the back of the couch,

'For now, it will only allow you to conceptualize the upper layers of knowledge needed to understand the answers to your questions. I will answer as best as I can.' He continued walking to the couch where her mother had been.

Where was her family? Ceres wondered, but the train of thought faded as he began to speak again.

'I am male because that is how you choose to have me appear. I am guessing this essence brings you comfort, a form of adulation, and

devotion that you need to rise to your higher self. I am the part of you that loves and knows you in dimensions. No one else can. An unending divine love that connects you to everything unseen but felt. Yet, I am neither male nor female. I am simply a visual representation of your Eternal Self,'

Ceres frowned and started to speak, but he went on.

'In the beginning, when there were fewer words, the understanding was clear that layers existed, and you were connected to all of them in separate but united forms. The Spirit is connected to the Spiritual during solitude and meditation. The physical, inactivity, exploration, and mental in its pursuit to reconcile the two, like a motherboard, convey what you do on a physical keyboard to results on a computer screen,' He paused, trying to figure out if what he had just said made sense, then shrugged, accepting it had and continued.

'When people think of a soul, they think of it as being disconnected and impersonal. It's not,'

Ceres thought about that for a minute. Her body felt light, but her thoughts were heavy. She had questions. However, they would not solidify in her mind.

"What is your name?" she managed to get out as the sofa hugged her tighter, but she thought it was a silly question once she asked it.

With both his hands hovering over her head, palms down, he said,

'*You can call me Tellus,*'

There was a growing warmth between her eyebrows, and it seemed to increase as he spoke his name out loud.

"Tellus," she repeated sleepily, and a small pulse between her brows echoed it.

The sofa was warm and comforting underneath her body. It beckoned her to return to sleep. But, instead, she yawned profoundly and took a lengthier blink of her eyes than she had meant to.

"So, all souls are connected to the Eternal?"

'*Yes, even if by the slimmest of thread,*'

"Like a spider's web," Ceres said out loud, primarily to herself, as she laid back down, pulling a Batman throw over herself for warmth.

'*Yes,*' the winged man said, moving closer to Ceres.

As the young woman lost her fight against sleep and closed her eyes, the Spirit bent down and kissed her in the center of her brow. Tellus's form disintegrated into a gossamer ball of silver light as he did. It hovered over Ceres for a moment before disappearing into Ceres, her body curving upwards as she took a deep breath and then fell back asleep. If you were to look at her from an angle, you could see the gossamer remnants of the wings protruding from Ceres' back.

Chapter XXII -Cardamom

Cardamom is rich in powerful phytonutrients and is exceptionally high in manganese, a trace mineral that helps the body form connective tissue, bones, and sex hormones. As a result, cardamom is the natural treatment for cancer, diabetes, bad breath, high blood pressure, and digestion problems.

In Spiritual Work: *The queen of spice is also the queen of love and lust. Chew cardamom seeds before speaking to a would-be lover or before an audience to keep their attention.*

After leaving Leatrice's lab that Saturday afternoon, Jean went straight to his penthouse condo on the 19th-floor of ARTS Tower. The older man was disgruntled as he hastily took off his jacket and shoes in the hall. Then, he made a beeline to the kitchen to retrieve a bottle of wine from the refrigerator. The 2500 ft² living quarters were a third the size of his home in Fort Pierce. Originally designed to be a second home for him, Esperanza, and Mateo.

The three-bedroom, two-bath, open-concept condo featured a master suite with a four-person tub. A dine-in kitchen with panoramic 360-degree views of the campus. The living room was decorated in light colors, with an oversized wrap-around white couch but no television. It was connected to a small library with a sitting area for Zaza and, beyond the library, a secure small research facility for the nights that Jean couldn't sleep. However, as beautiful and accommodating as it was, neither Mateo nor Zaza had ever stepped foot in it. And no one except Jean had ever slept there.

Jean wanted to drink. To lament. To be angry at himself for everything he had allowed to happen. Uncorked bottle in hand, shoeless and on the verge of losing control, Jean headed for his bedroom, where the only television was. A piece of furniture was added by Philia later on. Something Zaza would have never approved of.

Philia delivered the 40" flat screen two and a half years ago. Insisting that he needed a distraction from the ongoing research. Jean refused to leave the California king bed, which was almost buried by books.

When Philia stepped in, nursing him back to health while watching episodes of her favorite show, Supernatural, he was down 20 lbs. from not eating. Now, the quirky, often misinformed show about two brothers chasing monsters had become a guilty pleasure for Jean. Something to watch when he was lonely and needed a mental distraction. Jean placed the bottle of Port on the Bronze dresser across from the Versailles upholstered panel bed. Then, untucking his shirt, he picked up the remote next to the TV on the dresser and flipped it on.

As the 40-inch screen lit up, the septuagenarian picked up the bottle of Port wine and took a drink straight from the bottle before starting to search for the Sci-Fi television show. As Jean searched, he thought about his youth. He was around the same age as those two young men on the show when he and Esperanza started their lives in New York. However, unlike those young men, Jean Dieudonne knew nothing about the supernatural forces around them. Except he had a beautiful girl on his arm, who had a book only she could read, which gave them prophetic advice.

Jean had also noticed his beautiful wife's power of insight, starting on the crowded ship during their three-week crossing to America. Zaza was adamant about keeping The Book safe from prying eyes. Taking possession of the family's sacred heirloom under his advice was one thing. Letting anyone see its knowledge was quite another.

That first night on the ship, while everyone was on the deck, either enjoying or regretting their first time on the water. Jean held Esperanza tightly on the one-person cot the two shared on the lower deck. As regretful tears rolled down her face, Jean had promised her that nothing would ever happen to The Book. That no one, except their family, would ever know about it.

"And one day we will return to France, après we have made our way in America. And our parents would be so proud, you will see. All would be forgiven, mon Cher,"

So, they had kept The Book wrapped and stashed inside the bottom of their luggage under their cot. But that didn't stop Esperanza from quickly becoming friends with the cook who served the lower decks or making friends with the cleaning woman, giving them an extra blanket when it got cold. Then, finally, the day came for them to get ready to get off the ship. The two of them had been so worried about finding a place to stay, at least that first night, before they could sort themselves out. Esperanza luckily found a lost bracelet that belonged to a wealthy French woman. She was looking for temporary help, which they could provide, thus preventing them from spending any nights out on the cold New York Street. All without having to look at The Book once.

Zaza was 19 the first time she got pregnant. Jean had watched her bloom like the most beautiful rose that ever grew. There was no end to her happiness as she spoke of baby names, walking through stores to buy clothes, and waiting to pick a crib. Of course, he worked a lot back then. Still, they were so happy feeling the baby's movements, watching her stomach swell, month by month for 7 months. Until one night, he came home excited to have closed his biggest deal yet with the bottle of champagne in his hand. Jean ran into their apartment and found her in tears on the living room floor with The Book.

"The baby is not moving," she cried.

Zaza had been too scared to go to the hospital alone and had tried to consult The Book after failing to reach Jean. But it didn't help.

Jean had called for a taxi to take them to the hospital. However, by the time they arrived, it was too late. Sighing, taking a sip from the bottle. Esperanza would be pregnant two more times before giving birth to their son. Each time, they watched her belly swell with the hopes and prayers of finally having this dream come true. Only to have the dream die inside of her several months later.

Zaza grew weary of using the Book with each failed pregnancy. Jean wasn't greedy, but he was impatient. And the sporadic advice Esperanza was now providing him with the aid of The Book. Jean wasn't growing their wealth fast enough. Plus, it bothered Jean to be dependent on her. He had learned as a young boy not to depend on anyone else. Around the same time, Esperanza had gotten back in touch with her family. Unfortunately, the news from home wasn't too good; her father had passed away. So, it took her a couple of days before she mentioned the miscarriages to Maria Izabella, her sister.

Jean remembered the night he came home after the sisters had spoken. Zaza was sitting on the floor in front of the fireplace in the loft. Tears ran down her bleached face as she tried and failed to rip the Book apart. Dropping everything in his hand, Jean rushed to separate her from the Book just as she was about to toss it into the flames. Only half heard her scream about the Book being the cause of the failed pregnancies.

In the months that followed, Zaza was overcome with fear. She refused to touch or even go near The Book; Jean initially didn't mind. He tried to be there for her as much as possible. However, in a few weeks, his business started to suffer. A little at first, but then, very quickly, very severely. Jean had begged her to seek The Book's counsel for him. He reasoned that she didn't have to do it often, maybe once or twice a week. Jean, after all, loved his young wife and didn't want her to be hurt. It's an *old wives' tale*, he reasoned. Sure, she was the only person that could read The Book. But that's all it was, a book to read, words on paper. She has no real reason to drag them into ruin because of her sister's old-world fears.

Jean took another drink from the bottle of wine. Since the television show was failing to drown out his memories.

"Stupid suspicions," the old man griped out loud as he remembered the night in their penthouse loft in Manhattan when things came to a head.

It was the night of Zaza's twenty-second birthday; coincidently, they had just made their first million. Jean wanted to celebrate the fact that they made it through it all. So, they went out to dinner, and he drank too much champagne. When they arrived home that night, Jean had gone straight for The Book for some reason.

"We made one million, but we could have made 10 more just as easily," Jean had snarled.

Moving quickly in his black suit, Jean tried to retrieve the large book from where Zaza kept it hidden on the lowest part of the bookshelf on the wall across from the fireplace.

"*At what cost?*" Zaza had shot back, taking off her heels as she headed to the bedroom.

"*I know you don't need The Book. I have seen you do things without it. You use it to keep me low when I could be higher. Your sister fills your head with wives' tales about The Book feeding on you. Because she wants you to come back. The doctor said it was your own body. It cannot sustain life.*"

"*I am keeping nothing from you. You say it's a wives' tale because that would serve your purpose. You cannot believe in one part of The Book and not the other. That is ignorant,*"

Esperanza had been too tired to fight. Yet, Jean insisted, accusing her of keeping him on a leash. Then, he threw the blank Book at her as she stood crying in her long white dress. Esperanza swore to him that all she knew of The Book she had shared with him and had no extra abilities she was aware of. Pleading with Jean, he noticed active listening and people-watching, which helped her know to whom he needed to speak.

After that, Jean discreetly started paying more attention to his wife's activities. In his mind, he wasn't doing anything wrong. He just wanted to observe her in her free element. But Esperanza never did any of that Aleister Crowley, candle burning, pentagram writing, things that Jean had researched about, that other witches with magical books did, to access its power. Instead, she would simply sit on the floor by a nearby window and flip through the pages.

Then, a few weeks later, one night at the office, while Jean was feeling pretty low, a gentleman named Abdul Crane came to visit his boss, André Benoît Meyer. This man, like André, was an immigrant. He had made his way in the world and was now a captain of trade and industry. These men were everything he was inspired to be. So needless to say, Jean was thrilled when, only after a few minutes of conversation, Abdul invited him and a few other fellas who were doing better than him to join the two titans at the prestigious, men-only Knickerbocker Club.

That night when Jean entered that cigar-filled room surrounded by millionaires, many times over, it was the best he had felt in months. He knew he was meant to be there. Between the expensive cognacs and fine Cuban cigars, a new fire began to burn inside Jean. A determination to be one of those men one day. No matter what the cost would be. Of course, he never thought the cost would be Zaza's life.

Salty tears run down the old man's face, some hitting the bottle in his hand with a clink. While others stained the front of his blue-striped shirt. Would things have changed if he had known the outcome? Would he have seen David Coe as less than '*A man that men could look up to, to guide them when the questions were too hard?*

Chapter XXIII-*Spikenard*

Spikenard affects the three major nerve plexuses – cardiac, solar, and sacral. Spikenard can relax the brain and cardiovascular system, acting as a "strong hypnotic cerebral sedative" and a cardiovascular relaxant.

In Spiritual Work: *Spikenard is a classic anointing oil. It offers protection and purification for ritual work. It benefits spirit journeys to the Otherworld and may help those embarking on this last rite of passage.*

The second time she woke, her mind was still hazy. Ceres sat up quite suddenly. She had felt a rush of coldness come over her like someone had yanked her bed covers off. She half-consciously reached to pull it back up in the darkness before realizing she was still on the couch and had changed position. Diana was no longer at her feet but asleep on the couch across from her. While Magalie was nowhere to be seen in the darkening living room.

How much time had passed? Ceres wondered.

On the coffee table, between her and her mother. The carafe with the golden collar and its accouterment had been replaced. In its stead sat a golden genie-like lamp designed with intricate blue flowers. Streams of smoke rose from its mouth pout, filling the air with the calming scent of lavender. Ceres breathed deeply, turning her body to face her sleeping mother, feeling the loll of sleep. When she saw Astar from the corner of her eye.

It was not the Astar she had experienced in the Dream-cast, but a much older one with gray hair and a persistent presence. Yet, even looking at this older version of Astar. Ceres knew she was the girl who had suffered so much pain.

Astar wore an eighteenth-century French-style white billowing skirt with a blue button-up shirt with long sleeves folded to the elbow. Her gray hair was dreaded but braided into a single strand that hung over her shoulder. She had The Book in her hand. The pages glowed as if a light was emitting from their depths. Astar was reading something, and although Ceres could see her lips moving, she heard nothing. Instead, as read, Ceres saw flecks of silver lifting from the pages to swirl in the air inches above The Book.

The young woman froze, watching the apparition's actions. But her throat went dry, and she involuntarily coughed. Astar stopped reading, the silver dust drifting into the pages, and the glowing ceased.

Astar lifted her head and gazed at Ceres, her expression warm and serene. She placed The Book on the corner of the table, next to a half-burnt candle, and moved towards Ceres. The closer she got, Ceres noticed, the less peaceful the smile on her face appeared.

The apparition bent down closer and stared into the young woman's eyes. Ceres looked back at her, unflinching. Something in her gut told her she had to show this woman strength.

Astar seemed satisfied, even if it was just for a bit. Sitting down next to Ceres, she began to speak, never taking her dark brown eyes off the young woman.

'Yo te di pitit yo nou te demon. Menm si sa, yo te san Bondye. Madichon Bondye, pitit gason Èv avec adam yo'

Ceres had expected Astar to speak French, as she had in their previous interactions. But, instead, she began to speak in Creole, a dialect of Creole Ceres did not know, yet somehow, she understood.

'They told their children we were the devils. Yet, it was they who were Godless. Curses upon the Earth are the Sons of Adam and Eve,'

How do I know languages outside the dream cast, or am I still in the Spirit walk? She wondered.

Astar's voice brought Ceres back from her musing as the ageless woman continued her monologue.

'The place I was born in Africa is beautiful; they called it the land of Cush. My mother told me it was somewhere between two great rivers combined to run into the sea. Each morning, we would rise to rainbows overhead and eat fish as big as goats for dinner each night. She said it was a magical place created by a woman from the East. The woman already had four daughters, to be exact, and the land's population multiplied. She taught her children many things about the land and God. The balance of nature, love, and protection. I don't know what was real or not in my mother's stories.

Still, I kept them in my heart to return there one day, whether in body or Spirit. The funny thing is that I still have not returned, but that is by choice, unlike those poor slaves who were born and died on these shores, never knowing the land of their ancestors. Spirits passing on lost and confused about where they belong,' She stopped and took a deep, reflective breath.

'*My mother was beautiful and a gifted healer. Our village prized her for her beauty and skills, working with everything around her to heal others. My mother knew the plants and their properties. She also understood the best time to use them for the best results, according to whether the moon is waxing or waning.*

All this and more she knew from her travels with her mother when she was young. She had traveled through Syria, Turkey, and Egypt, where she had studied in their libraries and learned alongside the children of those people called Moors. When she came of age, she was married and had me. But before my second birthday, my father died from an injury during a hunt. Still young, my mother could have chosen to remarry. However, as a medicine woman, she had status and did not have to. Like her mother before her, she traveled to help local villages and teach others what she had learned.

My mother had heard the rumors of the invaders as she traveled from village to village, but her fear never stopped her work. She was a woman of unwavering determination. Even as a small child, I remember her presence's power over others. But, of course, she also knew it was dangerous for me to travel with her being so young. But she would have it no other way.

We had been traveling west to heal a Chieftain's son when we were taken by slavers. Once a prize to be won, her beauty became a curse as the male descendants of Adam and Eve tore her apart before my eyes, raping her, taking turns,' Astar paused and slid her fingertip down Ceres' face. A cold wave ran down Ceres' body, raising goosebumps on her slender arms.

'As their descendants had torn me apart that night, as you felt through me,' she smirked, *'my mother died protecting me from their abuse, not knowing it was my destiny,'* She paused, looking at the young woman's pained expression.

"Men are like that," she continued, not bothering to explain how she knew of Ceres' presence. *"They do not care about the purity of life. They are unmoved by anything except personal gains, unbothered by the chaos and death they leave in their wake."*

Ceres sat up so she could listen to the woman face to face. However, the apparition moved, leaving coldness in the air as she retreated to where she had previously stood by the corner table. Her mother stirred but did not wake as Astar picked up The Book again, absentmindedly flipping through its pages. Ceres stared at The Book, wondering how she could do that.

'*Even now, through the eons, I see the seed of him in you, in your eyes,*' Astar advised, gazing at her from a distance, '*A seed firmly planted by force; a seed, like the bite of the apple enlightened Eve, force us to grow in unknown ways,*'

The room would have been entirely dark if not for the light reflecting off the ocean cascading into it and the glow of Astar. As the scent of lavender perfumed the air, Ceres was sitting up, Astar's words echoing off the walls of her mind,

Finally, she asked,

"Are we not all descended from Adam and Eve?"

Astar's mouth pulled up at the corners, but something taut in her eyes and around the lines of her mouth made Ceres uneasy. She wore an expression that would make even conscientious people hesitate.

'*No, Adam had two wives. The pale ones I speak of are the Children of Adam and his second wife, not all, but some. They are the men who created the Abrahamic religions. They honor God and his wisdom by turning away from nature, by taking knowledge from women, by making us believe our place is on our backs and never on top,*'

"Second wife?" Ceres replied, confused.

'Yes, his second. Their books say Eve was made of his rib; Genesis 2 Verse 22-23, 'Then the rib which the Lord God had taken from man He made into a woman, and He brought her to the man.

And Adam said: 'This is now bone of my bones and flesh of my flesh; she shall be called Woman because she was taken out of Man;' You do know your Bible, don't you, girl?' she asked with a smirk.

Ceres shook her head in affirmation silently.

Ceres' head was swimming. In all of her reading of the KJV, there was no mention of Adam having two wives. Of that, she was sure. Yet, something in her mind hinted at a truth she could not identify. In front of her, Astar's appearance looked to be dissolving. Stardust rose from her incorporeal body and vanished into the ether.

"Who was his first wife?" Ceres yelled, getting up quickly to move toward Astar, realizing she still had so many questions and no more time.

'Lilith,' Astar answered with a confused look as if she expected Ceres to know this already, *'We are the daughters of Adam and Lilith, but that is only one of the names she is known* by,' Astar continued as she faded. *"Adam made Eve, not God,"*

"Lilith, Adam *MADE* Eve," Ceres repeated in astonishment. "What the heck is happening?" she questioned.

Lilith, Ceres remembered. That name popped into her mind as she touched the picture in The Book in Haiti.

'*It's in the first pages of The Book,*' Astar continued, her form dissipated. Astar tried to pick it up, but her fingers slid through the volume as her essence was now more air than corporeal.

"But they're blank," Ceres informed her, picking up The Book.

'*Not anymore,*' Astar replied as her form completely dispersed into nothingness, leaving an echo in her wake. Ceres reached for her as the air turned cold, and everything went black.

Ceres blinked, her eyes adjusting to the darkness. She stood where she had last seen Astar, holding onto The Book. It was still warm, but the burnt-out candle told Ceres Astar had been standing there for some time. Ceres flipped open the thick, embossed cover and prepared to go through the first dozen blank pages to where the writing started but stopped when she realized they were no longer empty.

Chapter XXIV- *Mint*

Mint is an excellent source of vitamin A, a fat-soluble vitamin critical for eye health and night vision. It is also a potent source of antioxidants, especially compared to other herbs and spices. The antioxidants in mint help protect your body from oxidative stress, a type of damage to cells caused by free radicals.

In Spiritual Work: *Drinking mint tea can bring you good luck and protection throughout the day. Sometimes, the herb will be placed under a pillow to induce a vision of the future in dreams and to protect against attacks of evil magic, nightmares, and evil spirits of the night.*

That night in 1978, Jean understood David Coe was a pastor and Spiritual counselor for many wealthy men there. Jean had never heard an orator like him in all his life. As David stood there, tall and poise in a dark suit, flooded with white light. Jean was sure he was speaking directly to him,

"A man was supposed to lead his family and guide them. Real men who are destined for greatness, men who know sacrifices are made to achieve greatness. They know their first purpose as husbands and fathers is to care for their wives and children as their guiding light. Men were given dominion over the world, and women were to support us. Too many men fell prey to letting the women in their lives control their direction. That is why the world is in the state it is in now,"

The speech resonated with him with everything Jean was going through with Zaza.

'*Yes,*' Jean had thought, '*Finally the sign he had been hoping for, a go-ahead to ask somebody about Esperanza's secret Book that he couldn't read.*'

After Coe's speech, Jean anxiously confessed to Abdul about The Book and the babies. But most of all, about how emasculated the whole thing made him feel. However, Abdul's brown face had brightened into a smile. Leaning over, Abdul shocked Jean by confessing he knew of a similar Book. Furthermore, Abdul was sure he knew people who could help Jean and Esperanza. At the time, it was the best news in the world. Abdul's confession cemented Jean's mind about what course of action he would take next. Suddenly, one chance meeting and all of their problems could be solved. In Jean's heart, he reasoned it had to be The Book guiding him somehow.

"God, I was so stupid; everything happened so fast, and I never thought anything nefarious. Of course, I was ready to change the world," He chuckled dryly, taking another sip, feeling a little light-headed,

"Who knew the entrance to it was on Canal Street? I guess that's why they say you can find anything on Canal Street,"

On the cold winter morning, the taxi dropped Jean off at the corner of Church and Canal Street. Jean had spent a few minutes looking at it. I wondered if Abdul had given the correct address. The place where the shop was located looked odd. The windows were blackened, and there were no signs above the door marketing what it was for. It was sandwiched between two colorful clothing vendors. Jean's first reaction was to recoil — tightening his black coat, fighting the gut instinct that told him to walk away. However, on a corner of the window, he saw the same symbol on the cover of Esperanza's The Book. It was there he met the twins for the first time.

Inside, the dark shop was colder than outside—the walls full of glass jaws, soaking animals and fauna.

The twin albinos had been mesmerizing in their white lab coats, and Keffiyeh sitting behind the low white counter drinking tea from clear cups. Ahkter and Mahkter were nice enough, although their yellow eyes were disconcerting. They had offered him a seat across from them and a cup of the tea they were both drinking. By the end of his second cup, Jean had felt an overwhelming urge to tell them everything.

The brothers explained because Esperanza had taken The Book before, it was her time. The Book was feeding from her, which her sister had warned her about. Then they showed Jean a Book that looked precisely like Zaza's except for the image on the front cover. While Zaza's Book had an emblem of a stripped Diamond with six stars around it.

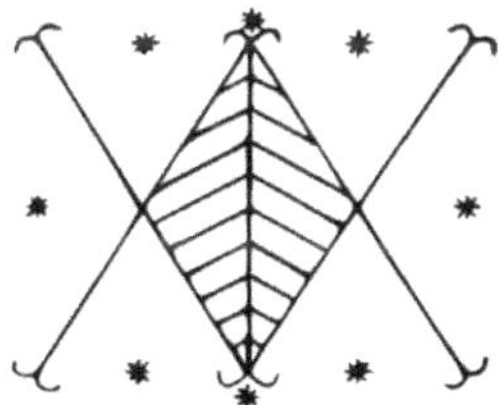

Jean was told that this other Book belonged to another man in the organization. The twins were also helping him learn to read and decipher his Book. That Book's cover depicted two arrows over a lightning bolt.

Ahkter explained in his deep, calming, accented voice,

"The Books' powers are perverse. They contain unholy knowledge made only accessible to women in defiance of God's natural law of male dominion. Such powers must not be allowed to remain only accessible to women."

Therefore, the brothers learned to create a potion, allowing the mother to give birth to a son. And through that paternal link, the father would access The Books' knowledge—something they had done for the gentleman who owned the second book. The next day, Jean took The Book to them without Esperanza's knowledge, and the day after, the twins returned The Book with a potion for Jean to give to his wife.

Mahkter said,

"This will solve all your problems,"

Jean never thought anything malicious of the brothers as they smiled, handing him the Amber liquid in a clear glass vial. He was too elated, only stopping to grab flowers as he rushed home. However, when Jean got to the apartment. Fearing her reaction if Jean told her that he had spoken to others about The Book. Jean decided not to tell Zaza anything. So, instead, Jean hid it in her drink as he apologized profusely for what had happened between them. Promising that things would be better, and they were.

A few weeks later, Zaza was pregnant. However, the two kept their excitement to a minimum out of fear. Jean hired a live-in Midwife, and Zaza was kept on bed rest. Finally, after 8-1/2 without problems, the couple dared to hope again. The night Mateo was born, Jean was on top of the world. Because not only did they have a son, but Zaza, overcome with joy, cast out the fears she had before and reread The Book. In six months, Jean made triple what he had lost in the previous year and a half.

After a few months, Jean returned to the store to tell the guys the news. However, they were gone. Jean didn't think much of it at the time. After all, he still was in contact with Abdul, who checked on Jean and Zaza routinely. During these checkups, Jean informed Abdul how Mateo was growing. However, Jean voiced concerns that even though he routinely had Mateo on his lap with The Book. It appeared that his son saw things that he was still blind to. Yet, Abdul cautioned him to be patient and take time.

It wasn't until the following year that Zaza had another stillbirth. Jean started asking Abdul about them. Slowly, Abdul explained,

"The brothers were only there to help you. As they told you, when you received the potion, it would bind your wife to The Book, and through her offspring, you will be able to read The Book, but my dear Jean, these things take time," He explained.

"Is there a way to get more? I mean, if she could have a daughter," Jean began to beg, but Abdul cut him off.

"If you have a daughter, the power of The Book will go more to her, and you will never be able to read it,"

Jean clenched his jaw, squeezing out tears. Slowly, Esperanza's fears about The Book began to return. They kept trying for other children, but Esperanza never gave birth to a live child again. Then the doctor told them she had cancer and tumors on her uterus the size of golf balls. Their relationship became strained again. And any love she had, Zaza focused on Mateo. This went on for 11 years until a miracle happened. The doctors weren't sure why Zaza's cancer went into remission. Nor did they understand why, after so many years, Zaza's sister finally got pregnant.

Mateo was about twelve when Philia was born. By then, they were already living in Fort Pierce. Zaza was full of life again and convinced Jean she should go home and give The Book to her. The Book should stay in the matriarchal line. Jean was not happy about this but wanted to keep Zaza happy. Jean remembered they had decided to stay in a hotel near the bookstore in Toulouse. It was the fourth day of the trip, afternoon in New York when Zaza called agitatedly. Rambling about how she had presented The Book to Philia and Maria-Isabell over dinner. However, now that she was back in the hotel, The Book awaited her.

At first, the sisters dismissed it as The Book's natural bound to the oldest daughter in the line. It was not until his wife returned to the hospital that Jean got a call a few years later. A familiar voice at the end offered his sympathy and help. Ahkter explained to Jean that the potion had an unintended side effect, which had never happened before.

"Unfortunately, because of the way you and your wife were using The Book before the potion, she was never meant to have a child. When we forced life into existence through Esperanza, The Book took payment in the form of her soul, which seems to be trapping her Spirit. However, with your help, we believe we can fix it and heal her."

So, Jean kept doing whatever they asked of him. Yet, Zaza never got better.

At 56 years old, Zaza was in hospice. The day the doctors told them she only had a few months to live. Abdul somehow knew and called the hospital room where she was in. Thankfully, his wife was asleep when he picked up the phone. By then, Jean didn't want any part of it. He was done. He had enough money. And so far, they had only delivered Mateo; everything else was a lie. He was losing Esperanza without ever gaining the ability to read The Book. Yet, he agreed to meet them just to get off the phone.

Jean met them with The Book at a steakhouse called The Oak Room. The four of them sat in a booth in the back. Abdul told Jean of the secret organization he and the twins were part of, run by elite men. Leaders who sacrificed as Jean had to The Sons of Eve, who believed their wealth could shape the world into a more Eden-like place.

"The world as God intended for men to rule." Jean laughed bitterly.

Mahkter was the one who reminded Jean,

"The Book will keep Esperanza's soul if you want to help us. The woman you say you love so much will never find proper rest,

Jean remembered the smile from his sharpened canines that made him feel like he was making a deal with the devil. Yet, Jean agreed to keep helping them, hoping they could free Esperanza's soul. So, he kept sneaking The Book back and forth to them. In turn, they gave him more potions and concoctions. Nevertheless, all the stuff they gave him did nothing more for her than to prolong her life or help his book reading.

On her deathbed, Jean promised Zaza that Philia would get the book, repair his relationship with Mateo, and protect him. She gave Jean a page from The Book, informing him The Book was connected to its part, and if anything were to happen to The Book, this page would help Philia find it. That was his only page; still, he could not find The Book to fulfill his promises.

Drunk and feeling even more sorry for himself. The old man fell asleep in his multi-million-dollar home, alone.

Chapter XXV- *Lavender*

Reduces anxiety and emotional stress. Protects against diabetes symptoms, improves brain function, helps heal burns and wounds, improves sleep, restores skin complexion, reduces acne, and slows the aging process with powerful antioxidants. Relieves pain. Alleviates headaches.

In Spiritual Work: *Love and chastity protection (when used with rosemary). Promotes purification, peace, longevity, and happiness. Place a small satchel of dried lavender under your pillow at night to help you sleep better.*

Ceres studied at the first page, studying the cartouche that was now there. It looked as if it was as old as The Book itself. Still, she was sure it had not been there before. Slowly, she began to walk back to the couch. On the next page was what Ceres assumed to be the writing, though she could not figure out what kind of language it was. Sitting down, she glided her hand over it. Murmurs of sounds seemed to pass from her fingertips to her mind, allowing a sensory translation. She *felt* the meaning of the words rather than read them.

'*Amore per ti*' were the words and the feeling. And she lived there for a while, lived in this overwhelming love that thing was given to her. It was a sound that pulsated in three syllables. And moved throughout her body. Each pulse healed her, loved her, and comforted her. It was a delicate, warm whisper in her ear on a cold winter night. '*Amore per ti,*' it pledged.

'*Amore per ti.*' It was just what it said– 'love for you.'

She wondered at her physical reaction to the connection to the words in The Book. Then she remembered a Bible verse. "In the beginning was the Word, and the Word was with God, and the Word was God."

✳✳✳✳

The third time Ceres awoke, she was no longer on this plane. Instead, she found herself in an incredible paradise. In the distance, a waterfall cascaded down from the high mountain and flowed into a river below. The river shimmered from sunlight, casting off rainbows of color while animals of all kinds lay by its banks. She couldn't identify the lush green shrubs and many crimson, yellow, and purple flowers surrounding the pool. The mist from the water and sunlight caused a rainbow to form, making the whole scene look like something a great adman came up with.

I must be dreaming about Fiji, Ceres thought.

She and Dax had been researching Fiji as a possible trip before starting college. Her subconscious, she surmised, was probably pulling from hidden memory files to formulate this dream.

Ceres mentally high-fived herself in the dream over her remarkable powers of deduction, even in a reverie. Although she had to admit, she was disappointed in her Fiji dream on one level. Where were the cute guys, and where was the beach?

'*No, not Fuji,*' The other voice, who she knew now as Tellus, advised.

Ceres tried to focus to see if he was around but couldn't locate him.

'*Focus,*' He suggested.

Suddenly, a great black beast appeared. The long, dark mane glistened in the sun. Crowning its black face with bushy hair fell its large shoulders, which stood almost the same height as Ceres. The beast glanced in her direction, releasing a reverberating roar, exposing sharp white canines. It moved lazily past her, followed by a smaller, less hairy companion in the course of the waterfall.

Ceres held her breath, frozen by fear.

Okay, not a dream, still tripping, she thought.

'*Focus,*' Tellus reminded her.

The Black lion paused and looked toward her. Its sharp yellow eyes stared into hers, giving her the distinct feeling that they had met before. Then, as did the lioness, it seemed to nod to her before moving on. Ceres slowly let out the breath she had been holding in. And decided for once, during this journey, she would head in the opposite direction of danger. So, she turned around and began walking through a path of lushest plants, whose leaves were large and green like banana trees.

She walked through the clearing just in time to see a blinding energy sphere. The luminescent globe felt warm even from this distance and comfortable to Ceres. She thought of the orbs she had researched that some people saw. Averting her eyes so she could look at it better.

Ceres watched as the sphere birthed a smaller sphere. And that smaller sphere split into two.

The words 'self-replicating cells' came to the mind of the young medical student. Finally, the two smaller energy orbs morphed into a man and a woman. The original sphere of Light grew brighter, and somehow Ceres could feel Its Joy from the creation. Ceres watched as he stumbled toward her, almost falling, and caught himself on her shoulders. The first woman breathed, opening her hazel eyes to the brown man who held her.

"Is this the beginning?" Ceres questioned silently.

"Yes," she heard the answer. However, Ceres wasn't sure where the answer came from.

The pair smiled with excitement and wonder at each other, feeling each other's faces and coarse dark hair. Ceres could feel their admiration for each other.

"Marduk," The woman whispered out of the blue.

"Tiamat," the man answered.

Ceres frowned. She had never heard those names before. Instead, Ceres noticed cosmic threading from each animal to its pair, the plants, and the woman and man. Like a thin trail of light that was interwoven and flowing through everything, all the way to The Creator. She followed them as they discovered their World, and time seemed to stream in years rather than minutes as she did so. The couple was nude but fearless as they walked among the animals together. Naming them, caressing the black lions' mane, feeding the giraffes, watching the birds in the sky, and eating from the many fruit trees Ceres had never seen before. She could feel the care in his touch as he ran his fingers through her thick, curly hair and kissed her for the first time.

She noticed Marduk was strong enough to pick Tiamat up over his head, was as fast as the spotted cats, and made Tiamat feel safe within his loving embrace. But the woman was wise, teaching him to see and study the animals beyond his eyes. For example, to pay attention to when the great black lions slept, how the bees moved from flower to flower, and why the woman thought certain animals would only eat certain plants.

Tiamat gave Marduk direction since she had a vision beyond what was there and could see what could be. She knew how to form large plant leaves to make an overhang so their nude bodies would not be wet from the falling waters. Tiamat showed Marduk love and compassion, always waiting for his return from learning about their land from their Creator. Ceres watched with the couple one day as the orb rose and disappeared into the sky. Tiamat seemed sad momentarily as Marduk put his arm around her for comfort. Then, in a moment Ceres almost missed, Tiamat sat apart from him. With the flat of a broad leaf across her knees, she pressed her fingertip to its surface and began to write — slowly at first, then with focus and certainty, the way a person records something they know must not be lost. Silver light lifted from the markings as she made them. When she had filled the first leaf, she set it aside and began a second. Then a third. Then a fourth. Each one she pressed into the bark of a different tree — one for each direction, Ceres realized, watching her move. North. South. East. West. When it was done, Tiamat pressed her palm flat over the last one and bowed her head, as if sealing a promise. Ceres understood without being told: whatever was in those four leaves was meant to outlast everything.

Suddenly, the darkness engulfed Ceres once more. When she reappeared, she thought she had arrived in the exact location, maybe another time frame. But here, there were taller mountains and none of the noise of the waterfalls. Ceres was standing on the opposite side of the river, looking at a man who resembled Marduk but was more muscular. She moved closer to the water's edge to look. The full moon's light was a great help.

He looked like he had some kind of makeshift book open by the river's edge. The man seemed to be mumbling as he made marks on the earth. Ceres watched as filaments of energy seemed to funnel into the patterns on the ground. The man cut his side with a spear and added it into the dirt. She heard the sound of a low hum before the darkness retook her.

Ceres was confused when she reappeared at the same stop at daybreak. Until she heard the woman shouting across the river.

"Adam, what have you done?"

The woman who looked like Tiamat spoke to the man who resembled Marduk.

"Adam," Ceres mouthed in astonishment. Then Ceres's face turned to confusion when she saw another woman sitting beside Adam at the stop where he had written the symbols.

Adam smiled, *"Lilith, I'm happy you slept well. This is Eve. She will need you to teach her."*

Ceres was unsure who looked more shocked at that statement, Lilith or herself.

Ceres managed to get out, "Holy fuck," before the darkness retook her.

Chapter XXVI - *Hemp*

Hemp seeds and foods rich in Gamma-Linolenic acid (GLA) like hemp seeds have also been observed to help people with ADHD, breast pain, diabetes, diabetic neuropathy, heart disease, high blood pressure, multiple sclerosis, obesity, premenstrual syndrome, rheumatoid arthritis, skin allergies.

In Spiritual work: *Hemp can intensify a vision quest when burned like incense while meditating. This is because it shares the same energy as clear quartz and is a natural amplifier.*

Sunday morning, Jean woke up with a headache and a renewed resolve to find the location of The Book after a mass at St. Anastasia. Yes, he was disappointed in the lack of results from Leatrice. He couldn't let that stop him from fulfilling his promises. He thought about calling Philia. However, he changed his mind. Hoping maybe she was sleeping in after her date. After a while, he found himself in front of the small desk by the window. Before him was a leather-bound notebook opened to a blank page. He was tapping with the eraser of a pencil in his hand and quietly repeating,

"May the God who created me take my hand, direct the breath of my mouth, and lead my feet where I may manifest my birthright."

Jean hoped the ritual Esperanza had taught him would lead him toward whoever had his missing Book. One of the few things his late wife had taught him was how to allow his mind to go blank, let divine intuition flow through him, and then take immediate, decisive action.

'The problem with most people,'

Esperanza was speaking in an unmistakable French accent. Sitting on the floor in a long-flowered dress, with The Book always in her lap,

'Are they asking a question but do not wait for the answer? Or people wait for the answer but don't take immediate action once they receive

the answer. God is always listening, and he is always answering. You just have to walk. Knowing where you are going will take you where you need to be.'

Outside the window, blue skies and cumulus clouds provided a calm, relaxing feeling for those living below; at least, that's what they did for Jean as a youth in France.

The old man sighed. *Such beauty had to be created*, he thought.

"May the God who created me take my hand, direct the breath of my mouth, and lead my feet where I may manifest my birthright," he repeated.

Pure thoughts were the key. The simple reminiscing thoughts of the happy ones. The ones that fill our hearts with warmth and unconsciously bring a smile to our faces. Jean thought about his beautiful, tall, slender wife, with her beautiful brown complexion and the black curls that fell in ringlets down her back. She was happy even in her fragile state after Mateo's birth. As she played with him in the crib, Esperanza kept him in their master bedroom. He thought about when they moved from their cold loft in New York, which had many unpleasant memories.

Down into the five-bedroom home on the beach and smiled. Esperanza had fallen in love with the Spanish-style two-story beachfront property as soon as she saw it on the cul-de-sac in Fort Pierce. The exterior was white and smooth, with red-tiled roofs and large arched windows reminiscent of Andalusia, Spain. A guest living room and a sunken family room on the first floor looked out to the beach, located next to the large kitchen that Esperanza loved to cook in. Even with all the money, she insisted.

Esperanza was only 32, and Mateo was 2 when they moved. The house had an elevator, essential to Jean because it showed status. It had large windows on the wall connecting the four bedrooms upstairs to the library on the second floor.

The old man smiled, thinking about how those years were the best of his life. Jean was no longer worried about money, although his relationship with Esperanza had changed. Jean knew she was no longer in love with him. Because Zaza no longer looked at him with hope, security, and admiration. Since she hadn't been able to have another child after Mateo. Yet, they seem to find a comfortable middle ground of contentment between the three.

They came to terms with her reading the book three times a week plus one extra emergency a month but no other time. She spent most of her time with Mateo, and he spent most of his time conquering the world. Mateo was a handsome boy, full of life, curiosity, and charm. His eyes were a mix of his father's blue and his maternal grandmother's green. Jean was sure Esperanza had been happy there. Jean had netted his first 100 million dollars there. By then, Jean understood it wasn't a coincidence. It happened the same week as her 33rd birthday.

As the old man took a deep breath, his whole body seemed to glow as he thought about that beautiful night and how perfectly everything seemed. His young son was six and adored him as much as his mother. While Esperanza seemed to be as pleased about the news as he. Even though she cared less and less about their wealth. Jean ran into the house with a bouquet. Grabbing Esperanza by her waist, Jean twirled her around as if they were children again in France. Her laughter had bounced off the interior white walls with their tastefully placed landscape paintings. Come back to them with increased joy.

"Mon Coeur," Jean had begged as he placed her down, *"let's rent a private jet to fly to Paris,"*

Standing in an orange saffron dress, Mateo jumped into her arms, asking for his twirl. Jean had happily provided as Esperanza kept those beautiful bright eyes on them. When they finally came to a stop, she confessed,

"I've already made reservations at a local restaurant," with a smile that told Jean there would be no private jet that night.

The restaurant was an estate-turned-eatery facing the Atlantic Ocean. The two-story structure was outfitted with a wooden walkway. It was decorated with clear strings of lights leading to a wraparound sitting patio with an ocean view. It boasted classic Spanish and Italian fusion, with interior décor and pageantry that reflected that mix. There was a wall of wine barrels, a beautiful flamenco dancer, and a pizza-tossing chef who'd delighted their young boy. The group had been small enough to be intimate but large enough to capture the restaurant staff's attention. By the night's end, Mateo was in love with the flamenco dancer, whom he had charmed into teaching him some moves.

What was the name of that place? Jean wondered. The restaurant's name came to mind.

'La Casa de Corsica'

He wrote it down and stared at the paper. There had been so much wine, laughter, and food. Esperanza had been right. She had a better birthday than anything he could have conceived. Jean remembered the Maître D's toast:

"May you always have the means to enjoy good food, be surrounded by good friends, have love, and live to see endless good nights?" Jean wrote that down, too.

How long ago had that been? Maybe twenty-five or thirty years. He sighed.

If only it were yesterday, he thought, swallowing hard.

If only he could lay down in Zaza's arms again and smell her hair's scent. If only he could touch her face again and tell her how much he loved her. If only...., a tear escaped Jean's iron will and rolled down his face, landing on the word 'Fort.'

He looked down in surprise, not remembering that he had written down the words Fort Pierce. He straightened up, put the pencil down, and wiped his face. He got up from the table and began to move quickly now that he had directions about where to go.

'*Action,*' the ghost of her voice whispered in his ear, '*was the difference between success and failure in everything, but especially when you were asking for Spiritual guidance; one must act quickly but consciously while listening for cues from their intuition as they move along,*'

Jean reached inside his church suit jacket, pulled out a cell phone, and called Shaka. The younger man answered on the third ring with no formality.

"I swore I just left your side a few hours ago, and you miss me already?"

****

Shaka Solomon had just ended a meditation session when Jean called. The younger man answered, half already expecting it. A lot had been revealed during their visit to Leatrice's lab yesterday. And the sense that there was still more haunted Shaka when he reached home. He had tried to empty his mind of any ego-based need that would have caused it by meditating. Only to have the word south, hunt his thoughts as he tried to quiet them.

Shaka moved through the living room and around the black leather sofa of the three-bedroom condo and went to the kitchen to get some water. His kitchen was the pride of his living space. He'd spent nearly twenty thousand dollars renovating and updating appliances and furnishings, something he would never tell his prudent mother.

"I do," Jean joked, "I was thinking about taking a road trip and wanted to see if you were up for some adventure?"

"Where are we heading?" Shaka inquired, then replied,

"South?!" At the same time, Jean,

"How did you know?"

"I didn't, but South kept coming up in my meditation today,"

"Well, then it meant to be. There's a restaurant in Fort Pierce where I want to have dinner,"

"What is that five to six hours south?" Shaka asked, drying his bald head with a face towel. "Do you want me to call Jesus and have him set up a jet?"

"Nope, I was thinking of going old school. Besides, have you looked outside? It's beautiful. We can do the American 'Sunday morning drive' thing,"

"Okay, old man, but I'm driving, and you're buying,"

"I was going to buy anyway. I'm a gentleman, and you're my guest. However, I'll have you know I'm perfectly capable of driving."

"Cool, you can drive over and pick me up."

"The French teach their kids they should always respect their elders," Jean admonished.

"In Ghana, we teach our kids to help the elderly," Shaka chuckled as he heard Jean suck his teeth on the other end of the phone.

"Any preference?" Jean asked which car to retrieve from his garage.

Jean's garage proudly held almost two dozen vintage American classics, from Cadillacs to Chevrolets.

"I want to say the 'Stang, but on such a long drive, we should probably take the Bel-Air for better legroom's sake."

"I agree with you there. I'll see you in about an hour."

"See you,"

Chapter XXVII - *Garlic*

Garlic has excellent health-promoting and disease-preventing effects on many common human diseases, such as cancer, cardiovascular and metabolic disorders, blood pressure, and diabetes, through its antioxidant, anti-inflammatory, and lipid-lowering properties.

In Spiritual Work: *Garlic can be used in banishing. Hang a braid of twelve heads of garlic over your door to banish jealous people and thieves.*

The darkness dropped Ceres somewhere further back still — further than the Garden, further than Adam, into an open land under a sky she did not recognize. What she saw next came in flashes, like a memory too old for language. Lilith still had not deterred from her course since leaving Adam's side. Three full moons had passed, each turning a copperish red as the earth moved between the moon and sun, and still the three angels followed her — advising her that she had access to all knowledge her parents possessed, and that only her counsel to Adam could rightfully correct this mistake. For three moons the Guardians had failed to convince her to return.

On the day of the fourth full moon, a sudden energetic change in the ether caused Lilith to seek high ground, and the angel felt it, too. Taking flight, they directed Lilith to a cave high overhead, away from the seashore. A seashore would be the grave sight of many Egyptians who decided to disobey God in the future.

Lilith had just reached the safety of the back of the cave when she saw a giant fireball fall from the sky. The three angels instantly created a barrier with their light. While Lilith created a second barrier with the plant vines around her. Lilith felt the water hit the rock she was in and lapped at the door's edge.

Further out, in another galaxy, the Omnipresent felt the distraction and significant loss for the first time. Most of the connections had been lost. So, the Omnipresent decided to return and review the status of Its first creation.

As Lilith waited for the water to recede, she discovered she was with child. Eve, too, realized she was pregnant, calmly and painlessly giving birth to her children. The Angels flew while waiting for the water to recede for food and dry wood for the fire that could be found in high places.

While the angels care for Lilith and her ever-growing belly. They continued trying to persuade her to return to her partner.

"We have to return you to your place as *Adam's partner,"* the angels pleaded as they blocked the cave's entrance from the cold winds with their luminescent bodies.

"Why return to a partner who sees me as less than him, listens not to my advice, and wishes me to be less than equal to him? So, he may dominate over me, always forcing me to lie below him. I, who hear the words of the wind and see what he cannot see. Why does he need me? He has made himself a new partner," Lilith questioned.

"That is not for us to understand. We only know your place is with Adam, and you must return." The angels demanded.

"The Creator has given me free will, and with my will, I choose to be free,"

The angels grew angry at her defiance,

"*Then your children will die,*" the angels threaten.

Lilith wrapped her arms around her stomach and cried. Soon, their anger turned to remorse. Because they knew that they had no such power. Plus, they had hurt the woman.

By the time everyone could see the ground again, both women had given birth to twins. The angels were overjoyed at Lilith's ability to bring life out of herself. On the other side, Eve gave birth to a set of boys while Lilith gave birth to twin girls. And while Lilith's deliveries had been painless. Eve had suffered much.

****

Ceres reappeared in another part of the Garden. This time, with The Orb high above pulsing in a rainbow of colors. Ceres felt the words more than heard as she reappeared on earth empty of vegetation.

"*You will be your own, speak, and it will come to pass,*"

The earth seemed to have changed a lot from just a moment ago. Now she could clearly see the ocean's edge where mountains used to be. Ceres was standing behind what appeared to be two separate families. Adam and Eve with two little boys. Lilith and another man with two little girls.

 "Dear father,

 "If it's truly so. If we both have dominion over the Earth and are equal, unbind me from his flesh as all other pairs are bound. I will find a place with my children where my wisdom is valued as much as his strength. Oh great, IAH, in your name, I use my will to be free of any being that would dominate me and treat me less than equal,"

 "The Earth is thy domain. By thy will, it shall,"

 Before her eyes, Ceres watched as the woman pronounced the Ineffable Name of God, IAH. The thin cosmic thread that bound her flesh to the man evaporated. Adam erupted into a rage.

 "You will allow her to take my children?" Adam contested.

 The orb seemed to look past Adam and at Eve and her sons. The Creator had given man intelligence, free will, and the knowledge of the balance in all life, unlike any other creature on the earth. However, the man had used his ability to create another intelligent being, not in harmony. And she had made more.

 The Creator already knew all that had happened through Its connection to all creation. Yet, It could not clearly connect to this new being

Adam had made. The information received from her was mercurial, though slightly more transparent through her children.

"Let her be. She has the will to choose. Her dominion and will are equal to yours. You have created a new wife and new children. A partner whose binding is stronger than the last. Beware that she too has free will and may choose another path if her knowledge becomes greater than yours." The Creator began,

"Ones not made from the balance of man and woman as we had attended. Although you have used your free will. You have broken the first law of creation. For this, I will remove your ability to create what you wish from The Ether."

There was a pause in the telepathic communication from the group for a moment as it seemed to ponder.

"The world is now out of balance by men's WILL. And by men's will, it will remain out of balance. Until men find the Will to rebalance themselves. One became two to live in this space. The balance is for two to become one and learn that there is no separation."

Then directing Its attention to the sky. The Creator caused the sun to hide behind the moon. Turning the moon red four consecutive times.

"Ceres...."

The voice came through firmer this time and sounded like her mother's. She cocked her head to better hear. Her attention was split between the well-built Nubian hottie walking toward her and the voice.

"Ceres!" Diana was calling out to her daughter, hoping she wasn't doing any damage by waking her up like this.

****

It had been almost two days watching her sleepwalk around the house with The Book. Carrying on conversations with unseen beings, drawing sigils around the house, for what purpose neither she nor Magalie could understand. Yet through it all, she wouldn't wake up from the Dreamcast, and her glow was getting brighter. Finally, after the first day of Ceres not waking up, Diane started to panic. But her Spirit told her to remain calm, that for reasons she had suspected long ago and feared, this process would be different for Ceres than any she had read about from the previous women in her line.

Finally, she and Magalie had gotten Ceres to bed. Helping drink mint tea to dilute the potion. Still, Diana sat on the side of her bed, examining her closely. She could see a dark, mercurial spot in her otherwise perfect silver-and-pink aura that may have been the cause of the problem, some kind of disruption to her energy flow. Maybe a block kept her from learning all she needed to, thus forcing her to remain in the Dreamcast.

The spot was in the center of her forehead, where the third eye would be. Diana closed her eyes to focus and directed all of her energy toward that spot. She imagined the flow of blue with silver energy coming from her and wrapping around the ball of darkness, swallowing it whole until it dissipated. The more Diana worked on the block, the more she realized her theory was true. The energy block kept her from rising to her highest possibilities, but why?

Her Spirit said nothing.

The more Diana worked on it, the weaker she felt, and the more a sense of dread grew. Finally, there was a burst of light that overpowered the darkness. Which caused Ceres to pop out of sleep like a runner's gun had gone off next to her ear.

Diana quickly put her arms around her confused daughter.

"It's okay," her mother repeated over and over again. "It's okay."

Diana could feel the force and speed of her heartbeat in her chest.

"It's okay, Cee, you're okay," Diana affirmed softly, brushing disheveled hair off her face.

Diana and Magalie noticed Ceres' green eyes seemed to glow as she looked at them oddly with the slightest hint of recognition. Ceres looked around her room and at her sister standing by her mom. Magalie's face looked concerned. However, her facial expression was not what Ceres was staring at. Instead, Ceres was more interested in the hectic, tiny solar flare-like tendrils of energy coming from Magalie. The flares were touching everything around Magalie. Ceres tilted her head, studying her.

"How interesting?" Ceres yawned, stretching as if she was finally going to wake up. Then, one long blink later, Ceres closed her eyes and tried to go back to sleep.

"No, no, no, no," Diana said quickly, pulling her back into her arms and forcing her to stay with them.

"Here," Magalie handed her mom the glass cup of tea on the dresser.

Taking the cup from Magalie with one hand while holding up to the drossy Ceres. Diana sucked her teeth at the sight of the cup. The cup, a skull head Halloween decoration she had bought at the dollar store, annoyed their mom. Tea was severe business to Diana, and this cup was not meant for a proper tea serving. Usually, Magalie would use the cup to bother her mother. However, this time, it was the first thing Magalie grabbed.

"You couldn't have found another cup?"

"Mom, it was the first thing I grabbed. Geez, I wasn't paying attention to the cup."

Sucking her teeth at Magalie again, Diana turned back to Ceres. "Drink, sweetheart. It's peppermint tea. It will help to wake you up,"

Slowly, with the help of her mother, the young Priestess took a couple of sips,

"I still feel so tired," Ceres managed to get out drowsily.

"You're probably tired from too much sleep," Diana answered softly, leaving Ceres to hold the cup on her own as she started to fix her wild hair, "You've been sleeping for a while,"

"How long is a while?" Ceres speaking clearer now, sipping from the cup.

"Happy birthday!" Magalie exclaimed, "Well, it's technically not until after eleven p.m. But I thought this might make you feel better since you've slept for almost thirty-six hours."

Magalie retrieved a small gift box she had sitting on the dresser. Ceres' face blanched as all remnants of sleep instantly released their hold on her.

"Two days, Mom! So, you let me sleep for almost two days?!"

"Now, before you get all twenty-first-century medicine on me—" Diana started.

"Maman, I could have been overdosing."

"You were fine. You *are* fine. Didn't know how long it was supposed to take. But I knew you would be fine." Diana countered.

"Jesus, maman, and Magalie, you just let her?"

"I..," Magalie started, but Diana cut her off.

"Leave our brother Jesus out of this; he was not here when I made those decisions, and your little sister knew we had to ride this out,"

"She's right, you know," Magalie replied. "Whatever you were going through, you had to go through it here. All that sleepwalking and talking to yourself was probably something you wouldn't want to do in a hospital," she finished, twirling her finger next to her head in universal sign language for crazy.

Ceres rolled her eyes at her little sister as she snatched the gift out of her hand.

"It's great-grandma's ring! Mom thought she lost it years ago, but I found it following you around the house," Magalie shouted out before Ceres had a chance to even think about opening the present.

"I hate you," Ceres teased, annoyed at her sister for doing the same thing every year. Then, opening the box, her eyes lit up when she saw the yellow stone and silver ring.

"I got it resized for you. And got the sigil you painted on the walls around the house engraved on it. I figured you could take the protection with you,"

"What sigil?" she asked, placing the ring on her right forefinger.

A sudden wave of energy passed through, and the confusion in her head grew with every word her sister spoke. Ceres handed her sister the cup and placed the box on her side. Rubbing her temples in the hopes it would alleviate her mental fog.

Her mother and sister exchanged looks.

"Why don't you shower and come downstairs," Diana suggested, "You stink. And you need to cleanse yourself of any negative energy, you know, that might be clinging to you. It is your birthday,"

"You do stink," Magalie added, turning up her nose. "Probably more so from the weird bath you had last night. Mom made me clean it up, by the way, since it was technically your birthday,"

"What weird bath? Why am I bathing while sleepwalking? Mother!"

Diana took a deep breath.

"Okay. We will talk about all of this after you take a shower. We'll see you downstairs,"

"But maman," Ceres complained in a manner unbecoming of a freshly minted twenty-two-year-old.

"Shower. Now!" Diana answered in a manner that left no room for argument.

Magalie's eyes widened as she made a face that said, you better do as you're told. Then, she did a heel-toe turn and started to walk out of the room. Diana stood up and kissed her daughter on the head before walking out.

Ceres sat there for a moment, looking at her gift. The wave that had flowed over had subsided. The antique sapphire ring had been given to her mother on her twenty-second birthday. The stone was large and rough, but it glowed like its center contained a miniature sun. Years ago, after moving in, Diana had been distraught to discover that it was missing. She wondered if The Book and the ring were connected, if, like The Book, his first daughter would eventually inherit it.

'*Your sister or you, whoever has a daughter first,*' Tellus advised.

She smiled, knowing that information would make Magalie incredibly happy. She looked at the engraving of the sigils on both sides of the ring. It was a heart with a grid pattern filling the interior and a staff going through it, while smaller, flower-like designs came out of the top and bottom. Looking closer, she realized it was the *vèvè* for Erzulie, The Healer. The Liberator of Hispaniola.

Ceres smiled at her mother's painting in the hall of the Black Madonna with new respect. She was now the Madonna's Prêtresse, here to help women in any way possible. Then, however, that smile faded as she remembered all she had learned.

In the enclosed space of her bathroom, Ceres could finally smell what her family was talking about. She reeked of the residue of a Camembert and Blue grilled cheese sandwich. It was so putrid the young woman even turned her nose at herself.

"What the actual fuck?" she questioned out loud.

Chapter XXVIII -*Paprika*

Paprika imparts a wide variety of health benefits, ranging from the treatment of rheumatoid arthritis and osteoarthritis to anemia prevention and even fuller, softer, healthier hair.

In Spiritual Work: *Boosting spell work, adding energy, fidelity, hex breaking, and love.*

Shaka put his glass down on the granite countertop and showered. He dressed casually in jeans, a sacred geometry print T-shirt, and expensive sneakers. Shaka pulled out an overnight bag and packed another set of clothes just in case. He learned in the five years since Jean showed up in one of his lectures. A day out with the old Frenchman could end in many ways. Like when they had to be Spirited out of Jordan by costly private security.

When his phone buzzed, he saw the text from Jean announcing the old white man was already downstairs. Shaka, lips pursed into a casual smirk, grabbed his bag and headed out. Shaka could see the Light Blue Bel Air downstairs through the lobby's glass doors. Standing next to the passenger door in an all-white outfit and straw fedora, the old man looked like he was on his way to the beach. As Shaka got closer, the nervous energy pouring from him confirmed this would be an adventurous outing.

"Wearing linen, huh?" Shaka asked, throwing his bag into the backseat and getting behind the wheel.

"Of course," Jean replied, grinning. "We are in Florida, going for a Sunday drive. That requires an all-white linen ensemble. You look like you are going to a rap concert."

"Is the required Sunday afternoon drive ensemble a French or American?" Shaka snickered.

"Ah." Jean twirled his finger as he got into the passenger seat. "It's both, well, no. The linen is American. But each country has certain clothes they reserve for Sunday's scenic drive."

"Scenic, that sounds longer than 5 hours?"

"It will be well worth it, I think."

"For dinner?"

"It will be amazing food," Jean countered, laughing as he patted him on the back, "I haven't been there in about thirty years. And I can still taste their marinara."

Shaka thought for a second.

"Do you even know if the restaurant is still open?"

"I do not know. I guess we are going to find out."

"Did you try Googling it?"

The old man looked at Shaka, confused. "Honestly, I did not even think to do that."

Shaka took a deep breath. *Yup, adventure,* he thought.

As the odd couple took the scenic drive from Tallahassee to Fort Pierce. The time spent between them was quieter than usual. Now and then, there will be a bit of chatter regarding the scenery or history of Florida and how the irony hadn't escaped Shaka, that he was a black man, driving a white man through the South.

"It's like driving 'Miss Daisy,' only the 2015 version," Shaka teased, "except I'm better looking than Morgan Freeman, and you're not Jewish,"

"Yes, yes," Jean commented with a thin smile but made snide remarks about him not being a woman.

That's how Shaka knew that the old man had something weighing heavy on him, and the closer the two got to Fort Pierce, the more introspective the old man became. Before long, Jean went completely mute, gazing out the window at things he only saw.

That afternoon, as they drove down I-95, Jean Dieudonne was lost. Lost in time, remembering mistakes that he had made. Things Jean couldn't take back. Plus, the people he became associated with seemed like he could never unshackle himself. It had been another dinner with another friend, who had only told Jean a half-truth, as he was doing now to Shaka. And gain his confidence for treacherous reasons, as Jean did with Shaka. That had set his life on the trajectory he found himself currently in.

After a while, Jean started playing with the radio,

"Do you feel like listening to anything in particular?" He asked, turning the dial on the radio from a rap song. Shaka reached over and turned the radio off.

"You want to tell me why we're going to Fort Pierce besides dinner? And don't tell me it's a gut feeling. Your gut feelings are going to kill me."

Jean chuckled, which morphed into a heaving cough. Finally, he reached down and took a sip from a water bottle on the floor by his feet.

"Did I ever tell you about Douglas Coe?" Jean asked off-handedly, not sure why that was the person he chose to bring up. In response to Shaka's question,

"No, who's that?" Shaka asked questioningly, wondering where this was going.

"Honestly, I don't think anyone, not even his wife, could answer that. Doug Coe is a businessman and an activist, sometimes a pastor to the average man and woman. But, to the people in the know, Douglas Coe might be John Galt. A man who set out quietly to make the right connections and positioned himself to control the world's motor."

Shaka's thunderous laugh filled the air above the two men driving in the convertible.

"Well," Shaka finally calmed himself enough to speak, "White men with money have always thought they were in charge of that, haven't they? Keeping the motor of the world turning. Isn't that why so many of them use the

Ayn Rand novel as their go-to guide for why industry titans should not be regulated by the government? Free to do as they wish with their workers."

"Yes, it's true, my friend, but Coe would have given Ayn a run for her money. He was such a small and unassuming man with a gentle smile. Who would ever see him as such a foreign affairs leader? So quietly, guiding world leaders to what end."

"Douglas Coe?" Shaka spoke the name reflectively.

"I doubt you've ever heard of him. However, I wager you've heard of the National Prayers breakfast they have every year in DC. Highly prized invites are sent to heads-of-state, Prime Ministers worldwide, including the United States president."

"Yes, the non-political but overly Christian meeting of leaders away from the prying eyes and the media." Shaka answer derisively

"It's organized by him and The Fellowship, an organization with no leaders." Jean mimicked quotation marks with his hands

"Really?

"I met him once, quite by accident. It was because of a random invite to dinner by a business partner of my boss at the time. An older man named Abdul Crane. Doug Coe had been spontaneous that night at the dinner meeting, but it changed my life." Jean smiled and patted the younger man on the back.

Shaka started to laugh again,

"All of that, just to avoid telling me this is another gut-feeling adventurer?"

Jean looked back at him with a shrug,

"Well, we will both find out what's south simultaneously."

"Have you heard from Philia since yesterday?"

Jean shook his head as he pulled his cell phone out of his pocket.

****

The ringing of her cell phone woke Philia with a start. It was the first time the ringing in the young woman had stopped entirely, allowing her to finally get some sleep.

"May the Gods smite them," she said softly into her pillow before looking at her phone. Only to realize it was her uncle.

"I didn't mean that," the young woman quickly corrected, looking up to the universe.

"Hello, *Tonton*," Philia responded sleepily, yawning. "Everything okay?"

"Yes, *Cherie*, I just wanted to let you know Shaka and I are heading down to the beach house in Fort Pierce, "but first, we are going to stop for dinner,"

"A big dinner," She heard Shaka affirm in the background.

"We're not sure when we will make it back up north," Jean continued through a chuckle, "But tomorrow should be a lovely day. Why don't you come to join us since we won't be there to keep you busy in the office?"

Philia pushed the phone away from her face to see the time. She groaned when she realized she had been asleep at 6 in the evening on a Sunday. While the old men were out enjoying themselves. She pulled the silk scarf hair wrap down on her forehead and turned on the Amazon firebox, which had turned off when she fell asleep. Leaving her TV on, just monitoring her.

The screen lit up, casting a white light over the king-size bed for one.

"Tu sais que ça aurait été bien d'être invité en premier lieu?" She complained about not being invited in the first place.

"Well, better late than never," He chuckled, "You can meet us for breakfast. I should be starving by the time you arrived,

"Breakfast..." the old man said slyly, running his hand through his hair. "If you take the jet down and the pilot can drive the car back, I'll fly us home."

"You are on your way to food and asking about more food, unbelievable," Shaka chastised him.

"No, uncle. You are not flying us back anywhere." Philia added.

"I've gotten much better since our last trip," Jean told her pridefully.

"Yes. I've heard," Philia said with a chuckle.

"What did you hear, and from whom?" her uncle asked curiously. "It had to be Jesus; he is a great pilot, but the jokes," Jean shook his head and chuckled. "Did you hear the one...?"

"Never mind *Tonton*. I'll see you soon."

"And breakfast!" Jean reminded her enthusiastically.

"Yes, sir." She answered before promptly falling asleep in the glow of the television screen with words,

"Le sang de la première femme est la clé." The first woman's blood is the key, repeating in her head.

Chapter XXIX –
Bluebells

The Bluebells are a flower that looks exactly like its name suggests. It is used as a remedy for leucorrhea and as a diuretic or styptic. Also, part of the stalk is used to make glue.

In Spiritual Work: *Add Bluebells to a garden to attract butterflies, bees, birds, or fairies. Or wear Bluebells as a hair ornament or a lei to compel someone to tell you the truth.*

The twin men meticulously packed from opposite sides of their two-bedroom suite in the underground residence section of the rectory. The suite was sparsely but comfortably furnished, as were all the rectory residences. However, the twins' living quarters were allowed additions over time and through many deeds. There were two beds, two high-back reading chairs over a Persian rug facing a fireplace, which vented through a system of pipes. The living room walls were lined with shelves filled with religion and occult books to read from and a small kitchenette to prepare food for each other. And their favorite part was that there were no windows, as the sun hurt their eyes and melanin-less skin.

The rooms in the rectory were ordinarily single. Yet, two separate rectory rooms had been turned into one giant, two-bedroom apartment for the twins. It was a gift The Society of Jesuits gave them for their faith, fidelity, and fellowship on their sixteenth birthday, Nov 27, 1942, after completing their first assignment.

Ahkter and Mahkter had to sneak into the Ashanti wedding ceremony of Iye Bako to taint the village's water supply. This would cause the sterilizing of all the town's women from having female heirs. The same Iye that would later give birth to Shaka Solomon. Still, their deed was only accomplishable because of Abdul Crane and a young, ambitious leader who would become friends with Jean Dieudonne.

Because of the sterilization, it was easy for The Church to get the Book in its possession. Even though they could not read it or care to learn much about it at the time. They went through all that simply because it was a source of power and faith for the people.

It wasn't until missionary tales of a similar Book being behind the Haitian revolution that The Church started to investigate. They use the artwork on the cover itself, its dimensions and description, to send out through their network of scholars regarding any reference to something that resembled The Book they had possession in any historical texts.

Soon, the news that filtered in was more than The Sons had expected. They were disturbed when they learned there were multiple Books, and they had played roles not only in helping in the only successful *slave revolt in history in Hispaniola*. This caused Napoleon Bonaparte's end and sent a ripple of rebellion throughout the Western Hemisphere in the 1800s. But another of the Books' caused the failure of *The Fourth Crusades in Jerusalem in the 1200s*. Another of The Books made the Great British Empire yield in the 1900s. When it empowered The Warrior Queen, Yaa Asantewaa, of the Ashanti tribe in *The Golden Stool War*. It was not lost to the brother that Britain finally won after the Church had taken possession of the Book from the Ashantis with their aid. The brothers felt they might be on the precipice of something as big as those history-changing events.

Over the years, the twins didn't only walk in unison. Frequently, they could exchange thoughts and feelings with each other silently. This is why the first thing they did when they returned to their apartment last night after the Phantom had appeared over the front of the Book, which had been almost inactive for half a decade, was repeat the location spell. The Brotherhood had vials of Mateo, Shaka, and Jean Dieudonne's blood. Hoping by locating them, they could figure out what had caused the sudden surge of energy.

Neither spoke as Mahkter retrieved the vial of Jean's blood and world map. While Ahkter retrieved the crystal pendulum from a small wooden chest. Neither brother was surprised when the crystal pendulum stopped over Florida on the world map. Florida, after all, was where his home and company were. First, however, they knew they had no time to waste. They needed the confirmation before Mahkter requisitioned one of the private jets The Sons had at their disposal.

"We should take The Book for quicker access once we have her," Mahkter spoke, not raising his voice, knowing his brother could hear him perfectly, two rooms over.

"Have you thought about how we will get access to her? Our skills are not exactly those of kidnappers," the older man warned.

Mahkter shrugged,

"Once there, I'm sure everything will fall into place; it always does."

Ahkter remained silent. Over the years, the twins had learned much. Nonetheless, Ahkter knew his little brother spoke more than he thought. And Ahkter felt there was nothing about what would come that would be easy. Because nothing so far had been. They were in unknown territory, dealing with powers they knew very little about.

"Brother," Mahkter started reading his twin from a distance, "I know we failed to recognize the peril of the subversive teachings in The Books represented. How they were slowly and quietly warding off the true teachings of God from taking complete hold of the Earth. Even more shameful, we helped move the knowledge that was once only a threat in Africa to our New World. But our Father knows God's will is with us. He knows these Books must not be allowed to remain in circulation."

"Then why allow them to be indestructible?" Ahkter questioned softly, "Knowledge that cannot be destroyed is impossible to contain from flowing."

'The Books and their current owners must be found and dealt with. To prevent the flow of knowledge to the next generation, thus halting its progress." Mahkter advised, "Then, their teaching can be undone through reeducation and assimilation."

It took three hours for the brothers to receive clearance to carry The Book with them, which was longer than it took to obtain permission for the jet. The two men were the only passengers aboard a G650 heading to Florida. Three hours into the flight, they redid the spell, this time only using a map of Florida. They were surprised that Jean was on the move, now registering Southeast of his last position. Florida is still three hours away but needs an airport location to tell the pilot. The twin decided to land at Daytona International, a midway point between his business and home.

"Which is good," Mahkter contended, "easier access to them,"

"Easier for us to be detected," Ahkter had advised as they sat inside the jet in the hangar, hiding from the bright midday sun.

The twins discuss little the young woman they were after and whose legacy they had stolen on the jet. Philia, most of all, was a mystery to them because of the promises they had made. The twins always thought of themself as honorable men. Only breaking their word, in absolute necessity, when serving their father. Such was the case with obtaining Mateo's blood. Still, the brothers were unsure if they could undo the binding they had done to Dieudonne's Book. If having Philia take possession of it was enough to open up the knowledge within itself to her.

The young woman had been born so late in her mother's life; The Sons barely paid attention to the second sister of the line. Under the false assumption, The Book's magic or nature had made Maria-Isabella barren. In all the twenty-three years, Mahkter was the only one who had ever been close to her. It was a week after the funeral.

Earlier in the week, Mahkter used an illusion spell to pose as a servant. More often than not, no one paid attention to a servant. Yet, servants saw everything. Mahkter had seen Mateo storing The Book in his secret drawer in his room. The brothers then waited 7 days for the power in the sigils to fade enough for Mahkter to return to the house. This time, as Mateo, to retrieve The Book. Mahkter hadn't expected anyone else to be there. And was caught off guard when a half-awakened Philia came stumbling out of another room. Forcing Mahkter to leave quickly without saying a word. The twins always wondered why Jean hadn't come straight after them asking about The Book.

"She's probably never told, Jean. Mateo took The Book," Ahkter shrugged, reading his brother's thoughts.

"She's had no recent contact with the Book. Her school records show no studies into anything esoteric or theological." Mahkter continued

"Therefore, we can surmise Jean kept his end of the agreement to keep her ignorant of it all," Ahkter said softly.

Mahkter sat up in the white leather seat,

"Whatever protection The Book provided by empowering the protective sigils when his wife was it is depleted. She should be as easily influenced as her uncle,"

When they landed at noon and rechecked his location, only to find out he was still heading South but was still North of them. Ahkter was sure Jean was traveling by car,

Across from him, in the posh white leather captain's chair, still wearing the same suit, Mahkter smiled,

"I'll get us a hotel room. I believe we should have all the necessities we need for it."

"You do understand the amount of energy that that spell requires?" Ahkter replied, reading his brother's mind regarding the invisibility spell from The Keys of Solomon.

"Only if we use it for too long. It will be just a few minutes when we're close to Jean and

Philia," Mahkter replied, convinced this was the right thing to do.

Although the brothers were very good at walking through large crowds of people without being noticed. Even though they were unique in appearance, once a person got a good look at them. Certain people had extraordinary senses. They could see things from their peripherals that other people don't register. They felt the presence of energy. Other people were mute, too. The Brothers had learned that people who could read The Books' felt the twin's presence like a sudden coldness in the air.

Ahkter sighed,

"We need a car with very dark tints. And preferably a house nearby, not a hotel,"

The house and an SUV with illegally dark tints were quickly provided through '*Friends of The Sons*. Jean had been a *friend* once, hoping to become a member. However, that goal promptly deteriorated when they failed to gain him the ability to read his wife's Book, and he learned The Sons had trapped his wife's Spirit in it. Whether Jean knew they had confiscated The Book without his knowledge was undetermined. Since the brothers had used an illusion spell for Mahkter to enter the house as help. Then, he switched to looking like Mateo when Philia saw him leaving with The Book.

They did know that Jean, who had once been an ally used to gain Shaka Solomon's confidence, was now using him as a shield. Forcing them to pledge to stay away from Philia and his son. Or reveal to Shaka everything he knows about them and who might have possession of the Book. This late in the game, they couldn't afford the extra attention.

The twins arrived at the nondescript house with their requested connected garage. With the help of a garage door opener, they pulled the black Tahoe inside. They didn't have to be this cautious with the sun. But they preferred to avoid it as much as possible. Prolonging time in the sun for albinos was detrimental to their health and even under a life extension spell. However, the men didn't want to take chances. Ahkter retrieved the only thing they had taken from the jet: a satchel containing chalk made of a dead virgin's ash, Jean's blood, candles, and other equipment they may need along the way. The brothers had thought it would best not to travel all over the place with The Book. Therefore, they had left it safely hidden in a compartment on the plane.

The older man walked into the house's side door as if he owned it, closely followed by his brother. Going straight into the kitchen, Ahkter opened the belted leather bag and pulled out a sealed glass tube that contained the chalk. He then proceeded to the living room, placing the container on a nearby mantel. Next, Ahkter cleared the center of the space of all the furniture. Then, he rolled back the area rug before heading into the showers to cleanse himself. In the living room, dry and naked, his loc hair pinned to the top of his head, Ahkter drew the circle on the floor counterclockwise.

Drawing a successfully working sigil was more than memorizing the circles, the art, and the symbols. It also required the proper education on what sequence to write the art and characters in and when it is best to do it. Ahkter thought it was fortuitous for them that it was the day before a full moon, as asking for favors is always best done when the moon is waxing.

Mahkter, meanwhile, started laying things out on the granite counter. The spell would take about an hour and a half from start to finish. The longest part of which was the meticulous drawing of the invocation circle. Mahkter tried to learn it but gave it up. The work for him was too challenging and tedious. Even though it was one of their most powerful tools. Ahkter, on the other hand, spent 20 years practicing drawing the circle freehand.

After Mahkter returned to living naked as the day he was born, his long white dreads in one braid pinned to the top of his head, like his brother. He went to the kitchen to get the candles.

"Place the four white candles in the four corners," Ahkter directed as he finished the circle and returned the chalk to the glass tube.

"I know," his brother retorted as he was told, placing the white candles on the four compass points and lighting them with a lighter. Ahkter retrieved the vial of Jean's blood, dropping one drop on each compass point in the circle.

Now ready to cast the spell, the brothers stood facing each other. The second part of the spell was the shortest but also the most dangerous. It was the invocation of divine beings to intercede on their behalf and grant them the ability to refract someone's eyesight. It was a physically draining process because as you received this 'gift,' personal energy would be siphoned off to maintain it, more so for Ahkter since he cast the circle.

The brothers closed their eyes, took a deep breath as they lifted their hands, palms down, over the circle, and began to speak the sacred words,

"O thou ALMIRAS, Master of Invisibility, with thy Ministers CHEROG, MAITOR, TANGEDEM, TRANSIDIM, SUVANTOS, ABELAIOS, BORED, BELAMITH, CASTUMI, DABUEL; I conjure ye by Him Who maketh Earth and Heaven to tremble, who is seated upon the Throne of His Majesty, that this operation may be perfectly accomplished according to my will, so that at whatever time it may please me, I may be able to be invisible.

I conjure thee anew, O ALMIRAS, Chief of Invisibility. Both thee and thy ministers, SATURIEL, HARCHIEL, DANIEL, BENIEL, ASSIMONEMT. That thou immediately comest hither with all thy Ministers and achievest this operation. As thou knowest, it ought to be accomplished, and that by the same procedure, thou render me invisible. So, none may be able to see me whose name I speak at the time I wish."

For a few seconds, nothing happened. Then, after a moment, the candles begin to flicker in the sealed house, followed by each part of the circle lighting up in the same sequence. Akhter's hand drew them until the whole sigil was glowing.

Then, there was a loud whooshing sound as the light grew blindingly brighter, eventually encompassing the men standing around it. The brothers silently screamed amid the potent energy rushing to cover their naked bodies with a shield. The ability would grow to cover whatever clothing they wore at the activation time. The light faded in the same sequence and activated a few minutes later, leaving them breathless on their knees. The men took a moment to catch their breath before they began to get dressed and pack their things.

Ahkter hastily broke apart the circle and replaced the rug on top of it, organizing the furniture as best as he remembered. Now that they had the gift. All they would have to do is say the person's name while they were close enough to them for that person's vision to never fall clearly on them. Then, they could speak additional people's names as needed. Or, in the most extreme cases, they cloak themselves from a whole room, which would drain them immensely.

The brothers recast the location spell in the kitchen and were happy that Jean had passed them. However, he was not too far South, traveling on I-95. The twins quickly got into the rental car with their things and went after him.

Chapter XXX - Mallow

Mallow is a plant that grows wild throughout North America. People use flowers and leaves to make medicine. Mallow is used for irritation of the mouth and throat, a dry cough, and bronchitis. It is also used for stomach and bladder problems.

In Spiritual Work: *Mallow is considered a reliable tool for attracting benevolent Spirits and grounding them to our realm for better communication. Smoke dry leaves on your altar when seeking aid.*

On the toilet lid, her mother had set up her usual birthday shower cleanse: Four clear bowls containing milk, honey, dried rose petals, and one with a mix of frankincense and Myrrh resin balls on a glass bottom and a silver ornamented tray. Next to a bottle of seawater harvested during the rising tide of a new moon. Plus, a bottle of champagne. The baths had started the last day of Ceres' first menstrual cycle, as had Magalie's, then repeated once a year on their birthday.

During her first bath at 15, her mother explained that women go through three stages in life: La fille -The Maiden, La Mère- The Mother, and La Vieille Femme- The Crone. During each stage, every woman had specific universal energies and powers that they could access to manifest their divine path. And it is in knowing where you are and accepting your role in that space that allows you to access what you need to move forward.

The Maiden- pure and full of life, she attracts energy. She is the cause of want and envy. Both emotions can cause her grief if she is not mindful. She is sensitive to her feelings and those around her; she is still young and has an abundance of energy that she needs to learn to focus on. The Mother is the nexus of life for a thousand generations yet to be born. She has become in tune with her intuition. She has access to the energy of creation: creation of life, creation of wealth, creation of a legacy, and home. And her sight can now see the path that could be followed. Finally, The Crone- she is the wisest of all. She is the counselor and leader, having mastered their powers through her transitions through life. Her sight is forward and backward, closer to the Ancestor than the other two, yet still connected to life yet to be born.

"Like mother nature," her mother said, "women have seasons, and if they follow those seasons and their rules. They will always have the best outcome in life,"

Whether science called it a placebo effect or the occult called it metaphysics. Ceres knew now, more than ever, that there were energies constantly around us that we were all connected to and could engage with the correct knowledge. To better ourselves and the world around us.

Ceres tried not to look at her matted, unruly hair in the large mirror. She stripped off the flannel pajama bottoms and white cotton shirt, along with the panties she was wearing. Turned on the waterfall shower that hung over the freestanding tub. The young woman adjusted the temperature to a level just above, searing for ordinary people. Ceres was not happy with the temperature of the water if it wasn't hot enough to fog up the bathroom.

She then pulled a removable shower head three-quarters down from the fall and rinsed off the bottom of the tub. Replacing the head, Ceres stepped under the water. The tired young woman felt instant relief wash over her. The hot, welcoming cascade of water pulled all negative things down the drain. She rinsed herself with soap before pouring the seawater over her body. While she visualized pure white light flowing from the bottle and washing over her.

After she had washed it entirely off with seawater, she used the detachable head to wash any remnants off herself and the tub down the drain. Then, Ceres placed the stopper in the tub to let the water fill it. As poured in the myrrh, frankincense, honey, and milk. The rose petals, she would use like a loofah, and the champagne was to rinse off one last time and toast to a great new year of life.

Her mother taught her the purification and attraction ritual when she turned fifteen. Ceres would one day instruct her daughters, too. Ceres reprimanded her mother for suggesting that she drink as a minor. But her mother, true to form, had looked at her, amazed, and said,

"The French drink a lot younger. You'll be fine." Ceres giggled at the memory.

She wished there was a window she could open to help with the smell but settled on the candles around the tub. The hot water on her skin had never felt so good. The bath didn't have to be any longer than 10 minutes. However, Ceres was known for falling asleep for half an hour or until Magalie got tired of waiting for her to be ready for them to go.

Ceres' eyes grew heavy as the water slowly rose around her, and the vapors of scented steam filled the room. She felt a sense of calm she hadn't felt in a while. A moment later, Ceres stepped back into her last vision. With the man in the garden, right there, reaching out to touch her face. She jumped, almost hitting her head on the back of the tub. Her heart was beating a thousand miles per minute as her hands clenched the side of the tub, looking around frantically. Okay, no one was there. Ceres did a mental self-evaluation. She had been in a hallucinatory dream state for nearly two days.

There would be some dormant side effects, Ceres thought.

"I'm fine," she said out loud, mostly to hear herself speak. *I just have to let it pass through me,* she thought. Ceres decided she didn't need to close her eyes for the rest of this bath. Going through the ritual with her eyes slightly open was a new experience. It took a more focused concentration for Ceres to form a clear vision of the goal she intended to create this year. Then, softly, she spoke the words of the incantation.

"A dash of Cardamom, two sprigs of Basil, and a stick of Cinnamon.

With each gift given with an open heart, my luck
is increasing by ten.
My Holy Father and Divine Mother order my
hand and help command.
Benedicito, Amor per te."

Ceres didn't remember how far the tradition stretched back. Nonetheless, she loved it. Finishing, she sipped the champagne and poured the rest over her head. She blinked rapidly to avoid having her eyes closed for too long. Exiting the bath, Ceres took in a deep breath and was satisfied. The bathroom smelled much more desirable. Ceres didn't have to check her watch to know it was already late afternoon. By Ceres' guess, Magalie made their mother wake her up. So, Ceres would not sleep through her birthday.

Downstairs, in the living room, the sliding glass doors were open to the eastern sea winds and salty mist. Ceres thought Magalie looked perfect in her white jeans, blouse, and long white knit sweater on the off-white couch. It was a birthday tradition for them to wear white. So, in keeping with tradition, Ceres wore a short-sleeve, bodycon dress she had bought weeks ago in anticipation of today, with a long, white-hooded cardigan.

"Mom, what's that smell?" she asked, sniffing herself.

Magalie busted out laughing.

"Valerian root," her mother called out. "I didn't even know I had any left." She laughed, walking out of the kitchen wearing an all-white casual pantsuit with a long, white suit jacket. A significant-sized quartz point hung from a silver chain around her neck, casting off specks of light as it moved over her chest.

"Whatever it was, could you please not do that again?" Magalie asked.

Ceres walked to one of the open doorways. The sun was passing midway in the sky on its journey. While cruise boats were making their way out to sea. Diana took a seat on the couch facing Ceres' back. Ceres stood there for a moment, staring out at the ocean. Then, she absentmindedly tapped the sliding glass door frame with her new ring.

For a while, no one spoke. The wind blew the curtains past Ceres' ankles; she sat watching them whirl around her feet. On the wall next to her, right above the floorboards, she saw the same intricately designed sigil *vèvè* on her ring. As she followed the floorboards with her eyes, she saw the small, impaled heart repeated at regular intervals all the way around. Finally, she stood just as her mother began to speak.

"I wish I knew more about The Book and why we were given it to guard, but I can't," Diana started softly, "We're not even sure where it comes from,"

"Africa," Ceres answered, taking a deep breath, "we can at least trace it to a medicine woman from the Oromo Tribe in The Land of Cush. She traveled with her daughter when slavers took them captive and raped and killed her. Then, they sold the daughter to the lord's house, where she, Astar, would be raped multiple times before she and her children were bought and sold in Saint Domingue. Astar is Cécile's mother."

"Dear lord," Diana said softly as she got up, "How far back did you go?"

"Far enough to be there the first time Astar was raped," Ceres answered, wrapping her sweater tighter around herself.

"Oh, God!" Diana gasped, rushing to her side. "I'm sorry you had to see that."

"That's fucked up," Magalie said softly, joining the other two women.

"I'm fine," Ceres said, letting go of them. Her mother took her hand and led her back to the couch. Magalie sat beside her, sandwiching Ceres in between them.

"The visions, maman, they were so real. So real." Her voice trailed away. "And seed from our pedophile, rapist great-great-great-grandfather, still lives in us,"

Magalie groaned.

"Forever cursed by the Sons of Adam and Eve," Ceres said quietly. "Marked by them."

"Ceres, why did you use that term?"

"It was what Astar said to me,"

"Magalie, get The Book for me. I think I left it upstairs."

"It's behind you on the end table," Magalie answered, pointing.

Diana turned to look and exhaled, knowing she had not left it there. Magalie got up and brought The Book to her mother. Taking a seat so that now Diana was in the middle of them. Diana flipped through The Book's pages until she landed on something written in French. The girls read on as she translated out loud.

"*And the Sons of Adam and Eve went forth, bringing war, disease, and pain to the earth. Using their strength to dominate and enslave others. They went forth with faith, as the Sons of Adam and Eve were the children of God, and believed they were right, as they had been given dominion over the earth. The children of Adam and Lilith were given dominion over the earth before she fled the Garden of Eden. Thus, her daughters also had the power, if they chose, to bring peace to all as they rise.*'"

"I'm not sure what it all means, but?"

"I do," Ceres spoke, cutting off her mother, "I went way further back than Astar, Mom. Back to the beginning to see the great breath being blown into the pair,"

"The pair?" Diana questioned.

"Yes, Mother. A woman and a man created together." Ceres informed them.

"Lilith," Diana said softly, more to herself than to her daughters, as she reflected on what Ceres was saying.

"Yes," Ceres answered, turning to face her mother.

"I had read the fables, but."

"When she left *The Garden*, she was pregnant." Ceres continued cutting off her mother, "With two children. The only ancestral line of the first two people on Earth. Carrying all the knowledge the creator had met for humanity to have."

"My God," Diana exhaled, her mind finally piecing together everything.

"Giant pause," Magalie interrupted, placing her fingertips against her palm. "Can someone back up? Who is Lilith, what Fable?"

"Supposedly," Diana started.

"Factually," Ceres corrected.

"In the beginning," Diana continued, standing before the girls, "God created Adam and Lilith side by side. However, Adam wanted to dominate Lilith, and Lilith willed her freedom away, which was her right by God's laws. Afterward, God made Eve from Adam and ordered them to keep eternally connected. And the Church demonized Lilith for being a woman that refused to be dominated by her husband.

While exalting Eve for her supporting role." Diana advised material.

"Shittt," Magalie cursed.

"Language," Diana reproached.

"This is not the whole truth." Ceres corrected.

"Excuse me?" Diana questioned her daughter.

"Adam and Lilith were the second generations."

"What?!" Magalie and her mother shouted simultaneously.

"Marduk and Tiamat were the first — created together, in balance. They gave birth to four sets of twins. Lilith and Adam were the last pair. In her final vision before the Garden, Ceres saw Tiamat write four manuscripts containing all the knowledge the Creator had passed to them, and gift one to each of her daughters. Adam stole the manuscript from Lilith and used its knowledge to create Eve — because he wanted a partner who would not challenge him." Ceres finished.

"Holy Shit!" Magalie whispered.

"Language," Diana reprimanded, although she felt like saying the same thing. "So, is Eve a Golem?"

Ceres seemed to think about her mother's reference to a Judaic mystical being. That was created with clay and animated with magical words on a piece of paper placed in its mouth.

"I don't think so," She finally answered. "Although she was made by man and what we call today magic. She was made with part of Adam's spirit. Not too far removed from the Creators."

"So, this Book belonged to Lilith?" Magalie asked, looking at her sister.

Diana turned around to face Ceres also.

"I'm not sure who, but it first belonged to one of her sisters, then one of her daughters. Lilith was given until a celestial event to bring back the balance the creator had designed for us. Or we would be removed from the Earth, and they would restart everything. However, the spawns of Adam multiplied faster than Lilith could teach them. So, we have until this event to finish what she started."

Ceres wavered, pausing to place her hands on her temple.

"I can't remember the event..."

"Relax," Diana said, sitting beside her, "You've been through a lot. "It will come in time."

"But Mom, this is important," Ceres pleaded.

"I understand, and it will be there, just as important when we get back from dinner for your birthday," Diana finished, pulling Ceres into her arms.

The young woman looked up to her mother, nodding in understanding.

"So, we're really saying. We are the same Bloodline as The Original, One and Only, two people on Earth?!" Magalie shouted out, standing up.

Ceres started laughing,

"Only if you believe in Creation Theory," The new Priestess shot back.

"Goddesses help us all," Diana sighed with a chuckle.

****

Diana had made a reservation at *La Casa De Corsica*, an upscale restaurant on the beach on the other side of town. The ladies arrived at the restaurant around 8:00 p.m. The three women were dressed in white as they pulled up to the front of the beachfront eatery. Diana and Ceres chose to wear their hair down and dresses—Diana in a body-hugging knee-length white dress with sleeves that reached her elbow. Ceres wore a long dress, also form-fitting but more A-line. On the other hand, Magalie went for white pants and a nice blouse while keeping her hair up in a ponytail. When the woman arrived for their reservation, the best table in the house had just become available for them.

The table was located next to the classical piano player, not too far from the indoor chimney of what used to be the music room in the estate before it was converted into a restaurant decades ago. Made the women the center of the room yet far enough from everyone that they were still very much alone. The restaurant was a fusion of Italian and Spanish, which was great because Diana and Ceres could split a Paella, a Spaniard seafood dish, and a yellow rice mix. While Magalie had a meat-lovers pizza.

"Twenty-two is a power number," their mother explained between the last bites of the stuffed salmon on her plate. "A sacred number like thirteen."

"Like Friday the thirteenth," Maggie teased, sneaking a sip of her sister's wine.

"Think more, thirteen Apostles...Zeus was the thirteenth God...thirteen lunar cycles...power, not persecution." Of course, the ladies didn't question her use of thirteen apostles. But, as their mother had previously educated them, Mary Magdalene was an apostle and the most important one.

The waiter came and asked if there was anything else they needed. Magalie asked for more wine for Ceres, knowing she would be the one who drank it. The women laughed at the waiter's knowing look.

"*Senora*," Daniel said in a thick Latin accent with a wink, "*no problema,*"

The women laughed more. The birthday dinner at the seaside restaurant had been perfect for the three of them. The moon was heavy and full outside the window. Ceres started to feel like she was done with latent side effects from the potion.

"You're sure you're okay?" Her mother asked, reaching over to squeeze her hand on the table.

"Yeah, I'm fine," Ceres confirmed, using her thumb to rub the top of her mother's hand.

Then, Diana suddenly jumped, causing both girls to react.

"Oh shit," She chuckled,

"It's just my phone," Diana advised, reaching into her purse and hanging on the chair. They looked on as she answered it with confusion. She had over half a dozen missed calls from Gerda.

"It's Gerda, Professor Gachette's mother. Diana advised the girls.

"Alo Cherie, everything okay?" Diana sat up straighter, feeling concerned. Gerda was not one to call repeatedly for no reason. Plus, she was family.

"Lord have mercy, Di. I've been calling since yesterday. Are you home?" Gerda, who was usually very calm, sounded panicked. She hadn't heard like this since her husband was sick.

"No, I'm not home. What's going on? Are you okay"?

"I'm fine, Di. When will you be home? Leatrice came down yesterday and needs to speak to you. There is something that you need to see." Gerda paused and took a deep breath,

"Her boss," Gerda continued, "has her...."

A sudden, short but sharp ringing in Diana's left ear made her sit up straighter and forget her friend on the phone. It was a warning from her subconscious mind to pay attention to any change in her energy or surroundings. The restaurant suddenly felt warmer, and once, the calm atmosphere now felt tainted with some kind of raw, disruptive energy.

Diana stood up slowly to see what might have changed inside the restaurant to bring on this uneasy feeling. Surreptitiously, she searched the crowd to see if someone had entered the restaurant that would make her feel this level of energetic awareness. Diana was only seconds into her search when she saw the two men heading to a table.

Chapter XXXI - Spanish Needle

Bidens Alba, as they are scientifically known, are natural antibiotics. Powerfully anti-inflammatory, strongly antibacterial, fights urinary tract infections, and helps with chronic diarrhea, dysentery, gastritis, and ulcers. Assists in treating inflamed mucous membranes in colds and flu and respiratory infections of any sort, sore throats from coughs, disease or overuse of the throat, and vaginal infections.

In Spiritual Work: *Spanish Needle's magical properties include healing, purification, and fertility. Dip a bouquet of Spanish Needles into cold water and use the flowers to spread the water over an area you wish to cleanse.*

Jean and Shaka had come around the bend to face the majestic exterior of the Spanish restaurant with great anticipation. Jean because of his fond memories of his wife and son. The only thing Jean had done right after his contribution to The Sons was make them swear to leave his niece and son out of it. Whether she could help with the mystery of The Books or not, she deserved peace, which Esperanza didn't have and may never have.

Protecting Philia and Mateo had been the last promise Jean made to Esperanza. However, Mateo stayed out of reach, making it complicated. Although Jean kept in eye on him through various channels. Jean had also tried to keep Philia as close as possible. Jean didn't know why he hadn't invited her to come with them when they had left earlier. And now, holding his phone, Jean wasn't sure why he had just asked her to come. Still, the old man could feel something was off. Jean sighed with deep regret as he thought about how he had tried to cheat, to learn something that only time and patience could teach.

Shaka, however, was starving. Jean couldn't believe the place was still there. The last time he had been at this table, Esperanza had been thirty-three and Mateo had been six, and he had thought nothing could ever go wrong again. The drive had taken seven hours instead of five, because Jean had needed to stop for pictures at the beginning — one last delay of arrival.

However, when they arrived, Shaka had to admit it was worth the time.

Inside, a Maître D stood between them and the main dining area with floor-to-ceiling windows that looked out onto the beach. The place was as breathtaking as Jean had described. Shaka was not surprised to find a table had just become available for them. The pair had that kind of luck. From the Maître D, a beautiful young woman with dark curly hair in a black dress escorted the two men to their table. As they walked, Shaka could not help gazing at the ocean beyond. For the last five years, living in Tallahassee had not been the beach life Florida experience he had hoped it would be. Jean was saying something about fresh oysters when Shaka noticed a woman at a nearby table glancing his way — the most striking woman he had seen in years.

He lost track of his feet for a second and nearly walked into the hostess, recovering his gait just in time to look back and nod cheekily at the goddess on the other side of the room. When she nodded back his way, Shaka thought his heart would stop. *He thought he might walk over and introduce himself*, but Shaka quickly changed his mind as he noticed she was sitting with other people. Jean, who had perceived the exchange, waited until they had sat down before commenting.

"That's too much woman for you. And you would never get past her daughters." *Daughters*, Shaka thought as he was taking his seat. He looked over again and saw the resemblance. Jean, as usual, was probably right.

"You know nothing," Shaka replied. Then, turning to the hostess, he asked, "Miss, by any chance, do you know the ladies at that table?"

The woman slowly looked over,

"No," she replied, "but I can ask the waiter at that table for you,"

"That would be great," Jean replied a little too enthusiastically.

"Okay, well, let me see what I can do. Your waiter will be right with you."

"Can you tell me where the bathroom is, Ms.? I feel like I've been holding it in for hours,"

"Well, that's not good for you," Jean joked as the hostess directed Shaka to a hallway further down.

Looking Jean straight in the eyes, Shaka warned the old man.

"I'm going to use the bathroom. Don't do anything except order food or drinks while I'm gone," Shaka said to Jean.

"Don't worry about me. I'll be fine."

"That's not what I said,"

"Continuer, I'll be fine,"

Shaka took a deep breath and walked toward the bathroom, knowing the old man would do something troublesome. But instead, a few minutes later, Jean noticed two women from Shaka's table of interest walking toward the bathroom.

"Ah," Maybe Shaka's luck with women was better than he thought,

What an excellent opportunity to meet the daughters before the mother!

The waiter's arrival broke his train of thought but sparked an idea.

"Good evening, sir," The young server with blonde hair introduced himself. "My name is John, and I will be your server this evening. Beth advised me that you gentlemen would like information about the table celebrating a birthday this evening,"

"A birthday!" Jean replied — exactly what he needed. He clapped once, delighted, "That's wonderful. But, before my friend returns, could you tell whoever that we will cover their bill?"

"Of course. I'll speak to the ladies' waiter and let him know. Would you like me to give them a note or anything?"

"Yes," Jean's eyes widened as he reached into his pocket and pulled out one of Shaka's business cards. "Tell the waiter to give the mother this."

"Of course, sir. Anything else?"

"No, quickly go,"

Jean looked up just in time to see Shaka exchanging pleasantries with the two younger women in white.

"Not bad. There might be hope for you yet. Although, I think I fit in more with them." Jean teased him with a chuckle, motioning to his all-white ensemble.

"Slow down, sir. Your wife can hear you,"

Jean stopped laughing and looked over at the table. He smiled as he caught the mother's eyes.

"My dear sir, I tell you no lies. Esperanza would approve."

"I'm sure she would," Shaka confirmed with a chuckle as John returned to their table.

"Sir, your message has been delivered," he informed Jean with a slight bow.

Jean winked at him in confirmation and pretended not to see the suspicious look that was now on Shaka's face.

"What message," Shaka asked Jean

"So, what do you feel like drinking?"

"Ugh, What message?" Shaka asked Marco sternly.

The old man tried to signal Marco not to say anything, but the smiling canary sang before receiving the message.

"Your friend is paying for the birthday dinner for the ladies at that table," John answered, the smile slowly fading as he saw the look on Shaka's face change.

"Of course he is," Shaka said quietly as he took a deep breath. "Anything else?"

"He gave me a card to give them."

"Mon Dieu, young man, you would be bad at war," the old man commented.

"What card?"

"One of yours," Jean answered calmly, sipping his water. "John, please bring us a bottle of your best white wine. I heard the seafood here is amazing," Jean asked, shooing off the waiter.

"Why do you have my card?" Shaka asked, genuinely curious.

"Why wouldn't this old man have your card? We work together, my friend. And you leave the things lying all around as if you want them snatched up,"

"Uh-huh," Shaka said as he picked up his water glass.

There was something about the mother that Shaka couldn't shake, like a magnetic pull. When he ran into the two girls in the hall to the bathroom, which now he was sure were her daughters. He had felt something familiar with them, too. Some kind of comforting energy, like peace, like the feeling he got at home with his mother.

Maybe she was why he was led to go South, He thought, rubbing his hands together for warmth.

"Does it feel colder here?"

"Not colder, just maybe less warm for you," Jean remarked.

Shaka chuckled, but Jean only gave him half a smile as he scanned the room discreetly. While his friend Shaka may have thought that what Jean said was the same, it was not. Jean had learned that some warmth came from life, light, and happiness, having nothing to do with the temperature of a room. And when someone with innated extrasensory perception, like Shaka, Zaza, or his son, felt a sudden chill. It was because some unwanted company had arrived.

Chapter XXXII –
Coriander

The herb acts as a diuretic, which can help flush extra sodium from your system and reduce your blood pressure. In addition, research suggests that coriander can help lower "bad" LDL cholesterol, reducing your risk of atherosclerosis, a form of coronary heart disease.

In Spiritual Work: *Coriander and its seeds are used for love, lust, and sex magic. Coriander helps to arouse your partner's desire, have sex last longer, and aids in fertility in women. Coriander also aids in divination and spirit communication. It Increases mental clarity and strengthens your third eye awareness.*

They were an odd pair: a much older white man in an all-white outfit and a younger man whose midnight-colored skin and towering height reminded her of Papa Legba, the intermediary of communications between the Spirits and humanity. A trickster Spirit that tells two truths for every lie when a mortal asks him for help. Papa Legba turned and almost tripped as he locked eyes with Diana; a stillness took over the room as she smiled at his misstep. He looked at her with the particular shock of finding something unexpected — and realizing he needed it. He smiled warmly and nodded her way slightly. Diana nodded back, neither breaking eye contact.

Whether they wanted to admit it or not. People make decisions about people they meet in the first few seconds of meeting them. If they were attractive, personable, kind. And for women on dates, if they are going to sleep with that man. In that moment, Diana could feel both of them trying to decide 'friend or foe' from across forty feet. Perhaps he felt the tingle of connection as well.

"Diana, are you there?" Gerda was asking.

"Yeah, I'm sorry. Uh, I think...." She paused and looked back across the room. But the man was speaking to the waitress at their table and no longer looking at her. "We're out to dinner right now for Ceres' birthday. Why don't you come over around 10 with Leatrice if that's not too late?"

"Fudge! I completely forgot about her birthday. Please give her my love. We can do this tomorrow. I don't think Trice is going to work tomorrow,"

"No. It's fine. It's a full moon, and we'll have a bonfire at the house. Five women are always better than three,"

She'd hardly even heard the rest of what her friend was saying as Diana was lost in her thoughts. She still kept answering yes to things, and those answers seemed satisfactory. They agreed to meet at the house to speak face-to-face and hung up. Diana had sat down during the call. Now, she glanced towards the table for the man who had made her lose her train of thought; however, Papa Legba was gone, leaving the old man behind.

Standing, Diana pretended to be looking for the waiter. She got halfway around the room before she stopped. For a second, she thought she saw two identical men being led to a table at the rear of the restaurant. They were tall and thin, with white dreadlocked hair. Their skin was so pale they looked luminescent in the darkened room. One of them turned and looked towards hers.

The moment Diana saw his eyes, she mouthed the words,

"Mothers, sisters, protectors all, guard your daughters tonight, I call," As she did so,

Diana imagined a ball of white protective light growing from her heart's center and enveloping her daughters.

His eyes were yellow, and he grinned as he spoke to the waiter. The smile sent shivers down Diana's spine, forcing her to look away. She could see a mouth full of unnaturally sharp teeth. Lowering herself slowly so as not to draw attention to herself. Diana followed the man's gaze to Papa Legba's table. She cautiously looked back and blinked. There was only a blur in her vision where the pale man and his doppelganger had been.

Diana swallowed hard. Diana wasn't sure what it was, but she felt it in her gut. Something wasn't right here, and she felt instantly trapped between them.

"Girls, why don't we call it a night? There is more wine at the house that Mags does have to lie about. And Gerda and Leatrice are coming by to enjoy the rest of your birthday with us," Diana offered,

Diana put her phone in her purse and the bottle of '*Cho, hot sauce*' she never went to eat without. Then, Diana started looking for the waiter so they could pay and go.

"You, okay?" Ceres asked as she rubbed her upper arm to warm herself up. She, too, felt unknown and unwelcoming energy starting the muddle, which had been a perfect birthday so far.

"I'm fine," Diana smiled as she pretended her stomach was not in knots.

"Ok, I'm going to use the bathroom before we leave," Ceres advised, rubbing her arm as she rose from the table.

She glanced around absentmindedly and stopped behind her mother. There was a dead spot. It was like a blur in her vision, which happens when you look into the light for too long and then move to a darker place. As she squinted, the feeling of cold intensified while twisting tighter the growing knot of anxiety in her stomach.

'*Look away*,' Tellus advised.

Ceres turned instinctively.

"Can you hold it?"

"Maman, are you serious?" Ceres looked at her mother, faking a smile, "Why? Do you have one of those cheesy singing waiters coming?"

"Yes," Magalie answered matter-of-factly, "but I'm sure you can go to the bathroom before they come. So, I'll go with you."

"Oh, yeah, and be sure to bring your vape pen with you," Ceres taunted with a roll of her eyes.

"Don't," Their mother said sternly, but the girls were already walking away. Their waiter returned and placed a new glass of wine before Ceres, pushing the half-finished one toward Magalie. He winked at Diana, who smiled curtly.

"Anything else I can help you, ladies, with?"

"No, everything was delicious. But, you know, I've lived in the area for twenty years, and I never knew this restaurant was here," Diana said, gazing out lovingly at the second-floor view of the ocean below.

"Well, are you happy you joined the family as our guest? We are very proud of our heritage here. The original owner passed, and when his daughter took it over, she proved to be an even better restaurateur than her father. So how did you hear about us after all this time?"

"A salute to her. She's done an amazing job," Diana lifted her glass to toast, "Honestly, I can't remember how I learned about the restaurant." Lowering her glass, Diana tried to think why she had chosen this restaurant where these men had shown up.

"Senora,"

Diana looked back up at the waiter standing there,

"Can we have the check, please? we are going to take this celebration home,"

"Your dinner has been covered already," the waiter said slyly, an excitement noticeable in his eyes.

"Oh, is that customary for birthdays?"

"No, I wish. That would be fantastic. But no, a gentleman across the room asked his waiter if he could pay."

Diana looked towards the other table as the waiter spoke, but still nothing.

"Oh, who was it?" she asked, knowing the answer already.

Before Daniel could answer, her blood turned cold as she saw her daughters speaking to the man she had been looking for, the tall, dark man she had dubbed Papa Legba.

"The two gentlemen at that table." The waiter pointed to the table where the younger man had returned as the girls returned to sit.

"Of course," Diana answered flatly, leaving Daniel confused.

"Hey, Mom, you got an admirer over there," Maggie blurted out.

"Ah!" Daniel exclaimed as if hit by sudden understanding.

"Ah, *what*, Daniel?" Ceres asked.

"Nothing," her mother answered quickly.

"Nothing," Daniel agreed, following Diana's lead.

"Uh-huh." Magalie and Ceres answered unanimously as they took their seats,

"Hello, admirer, at one o'clock," Maggie reiterated. "And for an old guy, he's not bad-looking."

"Ceres, could we carve the cake back at the house?"

"*Oui maman*, that's fine. The wine's better at home anyway."

****

As the brothers drove to the restaurant in the illegally tinted SUV. Mahkter remarked,

"It's a full moon. That's always been a good sign for us,"

"Full moons are where pagans' powers lie, too," The eldest brother warned.

"Maybe you should go in as a servant first. See who is there. Before we both go in," Ahkter suggested.

"It only works for 20 mins at a time. It's too draining. It will be better if we both go in. Jean will not expect us. Nor see us if we stay out of sight."

"Unless Philia is about to sense both of us. Then we both will be drained from the cloaking spell."

"Even if Philia could, she would not know what to make of it,"

Ahkter stayed quiet, but he knew his younger brother felt his disapproval of him taking this lightly. 15 minutes later, Ahkter and Mahkter were surprised to be pulling up to a restaurant, which appeared full. The older brother groaned. The whole situation was going to be an energy drain. As the Black SUV made its way around. Mahkter spotted the Baby Blue Bel-Air parked auspiciously in front of the restaurant. And both men knew the car instantly belonged to Jean Dieudonne.

Mahkter smiled,

"Perfect, he is having dinner with his niece. We may not have to use the spell at all. We can wait for the perfect opportunity to put something in his drink. Then, once he's incapacitated, we could help her with him to the car and take both."

"Where would we take them? His home would be out of the question. We do not know the effects she has on the sigils now that she is of age,"

Unlike traditional homes, Jean Dieudonne had learned how to use protection sigils from his wife during the beginning of the end of his wife's mortal life. Jean had placed sigils around his residences and businesses. Thus, preventing all magical things meant to harm him from entering those places.

Mahkter pulled out his phone.

"I'll text the pilot to move the plane to an airport nearby and requisite a hotel with a first-floor room. We'll use just enough herbs on her to keep her walking. Wait there for the plane to land."

"Sounds simple enough," Ahkter agreed reflectively, "tell the pilot we might need a support team. This might be more draining than we had originally anticipated,"

"We've handled a lot more dangerous situations than this," Mahkter responded, making the call.

"This is unlike anything we've dealt with before," Ahkter said softly.

Once Mahkter was done, the men entered the restaurant's front door.

The brothers walked into the Olive-leaf vine-designed frosted glass doors. A crowd of people dispersed around faux trees adorned with twinkling white lights. The crowd reacted to them like curtains parting to allow a cold breeze in on a hot summer day. The patrons turned around to look at them and forgot they had seen the odd-looking pair as quickly as they had seen them. In times like this, Ahkter was the one who spoke.

Some time ago, his little brother had decided to sharpen his canines. However, this was the only distinguishing trait between the two, as small of a distinction as the sharpened teeth were. It left Mahkter a more memorable person than either would like. Ahkter walked up to the maître d' with a gentle smile and asked for a table for two. The young man smiled at Ahkter, never once taken back by the fact that the albino with yellow eyes seemed to be something out of fiction.

Luckily, a table had just become available for them.

As the two men in dark suits approached the corner, Ahkter was hit with a sudden soft but power-repelling energy. He slowed to see the young woman coming from a corridor, wearing white pants and a white blouse. As she passed, Ahkter felt her energy push him away. Yet, she didn't seem to see him. Instead, she smiled at someone ahead without ever looking at the twins. Or the approaching maître d' as their host crossed her path without incident. Ahkter stopped. A second later, another younger woman came out of the hall, following the first. The second one paused momentarily, rubbing her arm as if she felt a chill.

Ahkter held his breath, feeling a wave of repelling energy emanating from her. Mahkter, who was paying no attention to the women, walked past his brother following the maître d'. He could hear his brother's voice advising him to relax.

"Your anxiety is so high, any more could feel it," Mahkter telepathically advised.

"Something is not right here," His brother replied silently.

When their host walked them around Jean's table with no incident. Mahkter looked back at his brother with a smile.

"Where is Philia?" Ahkter whispered.

A moment later, Shaka emerged from the corridor. The two young women had come from and sat next to Jean. Quickly, Ahkter grabbed his brother and cast the invisibility spell. Although, the bigger man would still be able to see a sort of haze in his vision. He could not see the twins enough to describe them to Jean.

"Why is Shaka here?" Mahkter spoke, finally sounding anxious.

"If she is not here, we need to leave and rethink. I can't keep this spell going too long," Ahkter replied, hurrying with his brother to the corner table the host was taking them to. He knew he could not keep this spell up long.

No sooner had he spoken. He saw a table where the two women that had made him were sitting. Joined by a third, seemingly younger, looked directly at the twins.

"Holy Father," Ahkter cursed, hastily cloaking them from the restaurant.

Chapter XXXIII –
Mugwort

Mugwort has historically been used as an herbal inhibitor for women's menstrual cycles and helps provide menopause relief. It's also used to reverse breech birth position, soothe and treat joint pain, and attack cancerous cells and malaria.

In Spiritual Work: *Mugwort is a visionary herb and induces psychic dreams and prophetic visions. Mugwort can be absorbed trans-dermally through lotions and can also be smoked.*

"Will there be cake?" That was Maggie, concerned only because she wanted cake, and her sister's birthday offered the perfect excuse.

"I can add a cake to your bill and pack it to go," Daniel suggested.

"Nah," Ceres answered. "That's too much, maman."

"That would be perfect," Diana answered flatly. She didn't want to accept anything from them. But Diana also didn't want to say anything in front of the girls,

"Wonderful," the waiter said with a clap. "You can choose chocolate and churros cakes or *Triple Chocolate de Tierra*."

"Whatever is the most expensive thing you have available right now," Diana answered, cutting him off. At this point, Diana had decided: if she was in for an inch, she was in for the mile.

"Maman!" Ceres called out to her mother, feeling she was going too far.

"*Fantastico*," Daniel confirmed and walked away with her order.

"Maman, what are you doing? There is no reason for us to spend money on a whole cake. No one is going to eat it."

"Speak for yourself," Magalie retorted. Ceres rolled her eyes at her younger sister.

"Ladies," Their mother began. "Please raise your glass to salute our benefactor for the evening—my admirer at one o'clock." Then, with the most fictitious smile she could muster, she raised a glass in the direction of the man with the midnight skin, looking at them earnestly, confused.

Ceres and Magalie exchanged looks; both felt like something was off. But the girls turned around and raised their glasses to the man. Ceres was surprised to see it was the same dark man she had encountered in the hall on the way to the bathroom. She looked back and forth between this man and her mother. There was something there that she couldn't place her finger on. Then, the thought was interrupted when the waiter returned with a white box and put it on the table.

"You're amazing. Tip yourself well," Magalie said to Daniel, grabbing the cake off the table.

"Oh, yes," Daniel said, taking something out of his pocket. "The gentleman told me to give this to you." He handed Diana a business card with Shaka's information and number.

Diana looked at the card, then at Shaka Solomon. Now, she had a name for the man she'd previously called Papa Legba. At the same time, Diana felt the cold energy of the men behind her, whom Diana knew were watching his table. Something wasn't right here; she was sure of it and didn't want any part of it. Diana made sure Shaka saw her put the card down on the table as Diana walked away. *Whether Friend or Foe*, she decided she didn't want any part of it in that instance.

The mother of two watched as the older white man burst into laughter, almost spilling wine on himself at her actions. He reached up to pat his friend on the back in consolation. Shaka lifted his glass at her in salute. However, even from this far, Diana could tell that it was not a gesture of surrender but a strategic re-evaluation. Not even glancing in the two men's direction. Diana walked past them with the grace of a model on the catwalk out the door. Ceres followed her mother's lead but nodded with a smile towards the gentlemen as she walked out the door quietly.

On the other hand, Magalie decided to go to their table with cake in hand. She kissed them on the cheek and introduced herself; their mother groaned when she saw it. Ceres started to giggle, but it changed midway to her clearing her throat when her mother looked back at her.

"I'm going to leave your sister right here," Diana threatened as they reached the valet and handed him the valet ticket for her Wrangler.

"She'll end up getting a ride home from them, and then they'll know where we live," her oldest daughter cautioned.

Maggie strolled out the restaurant doors, and her eyes went straight to a powder Blue Chevy Bel Air parked in the restaurant carport, "Nice!" she exclaimed.

Ceres looked at her and placed her hands in a prayer position, parodying a thank-you speech,

"Thanks for making my ultimate birthday wish come true. I have always wanted to be an only child, and when Mom kills you tonight, that wish will finally come true."

"Maman, you still love me, right?" Magalie asked, walking over to her mother with open arms and a mischievous grin, begging for a hug.

"Ask me after I've had more wine," her mother called back while walking to their black Wrangler, which was pulling up.

Ceres opened the back door for her sister to get in with the cake as she sat in the front.

"Maman, what was that about back there?" Ceres asked, looking straight at the large full moon hanging in the sky before them as they started toward home.

"Some hot old guy thinks mom is hot too!" Magalie answered from the back.

"Mom *is* hot! And she's not that old," Ceres chuckled.

Diana rolled her eyes at her oldest daughter as she sucked her teeth.

"Maman, seriously," Ceres continued, "That was weird. I'm used to us getting free things from people, but those men felt different ...."

"I felt it, too. Something tells me we will meet those men again."

"Oh, definitely," Magalie concurred, "I think he's like Ceres, same vibe, same extra thingy,"

"What? What do you mean?" Diana's knee-jerk reaction to such an unexpected statement from her youngest child was almost confrontational.

"There've only been women Prêtresses as far as I know, and all the ones I know who are alive are in this car."

"You always said there is much you don't know, and Dutty Boukman was male," Magalie reminded her.

"That's true, but...."

"How do you know all that?" Ceres asked before the conversation got off track.

"Well, if he's not a Priest of the arts, he's pretty close to it. He has the same *je ne sais quoi* as us. You know, the whole soul glow thing," Magalie said, placing the cake safely beside her.

"You mean he has the same aura as us."

"No, Mom," Magalie replied with exasperation in her voice. Her perfectly shaped eyebrows furrowed like she was trying to figure out the right words.

"Auras are more like light emanating from our physical bodies. It comes from the cells of our bodies reacting to our constant train of thought and actions. The chemical reactions produce energies we can all learn to see with practice, right? You're in love, and boom, your aura appears red. That man's glow was intense and golden. It's the glow some people have when they are born with a fully realized soul connected to the Eternal. Not many people have that. Especially the intensity of the aura you and Mom have. I'm guessing it's because most people aren't that Spiritually advanced. His aura was bright but seemed trapped like vapers only coming fuming off his shoulders since they can't flow freely around him."

"How the fuck do you know all that?" Ceres suddenly shouted, sending both other women into shocked silence,

"I'm sorry, I'm sorry, I don't know what came over me. It's hot in here, isn't it?" shaking herself, Ceres lowered the window.

"Nah, not really," her sister advised, looking at her mom in the rearview mirror questioningly.

Diana looked at Magalie, then over at Ceres, whose energy looked like the molten surface of the sun. She could feel the change, and she needed to get home quickly.

"Well, to answer your question," Magalie shrugged, "I don't know. I saw it when we passed him in the hall of the bathroom. I thought you saw, too, and that's why we were teasing their table."

"I wasn't paying attention," Ceres replied.

Something else, something darker, was pulling my attention. Ceres thought but said nothing else. She took off a Black Tourmaline and Quartz pendant on a silver necklace she was wearing, feeling uncomfortable by the weight of the stones. Ceres placed the chain in the tray on the dashboard, breathing as slowly as possible. She clenched and unclenched her fist, trying to manage this turbulent feeling inside her.

"Well, neither did Mommy this time. She was too busy *not* looking directly at how hot he was."

"You know I don't like flashy men," Diana answered calmly.

She kept her eyes on the road as Diana moved quickly through the light traffic. The time on the radio read 10:30. 30 mins before Ceres' 22nd birthday.

"And, anyway, you're not completely done with your transformation yet," Magalie contended to her sister, casually taking her vape pen out of her jacket pocket and inhaling.

"Whatever," Ceres snapped.

Diana didn't tell them she hadn't even thought to read Shaka and his dinner companion. She had been too distracted by the feeling of danger, breathing down her neck. And that Magalie could do it instinctively had Diana's mind spinning. The older woman knew that in history, there had been times when more than one person could simultaneously access the power of The Book. That second person was called a Seer. A Seer was born once every how many generations? Diana couldn't recall. Her memory was not as eidetic as a few weeks ago.

They are brought into existence as vessels to help the Priestess see more than she could handle, she thought, but...dammit, Diana couldn't remember anymore. She needed to get home fast and read The Book.

As they pulled into the softly lit, circular driveway, the full moon hanging heavy overhead, another black SUV was already there. The calm, salted sea wind that blew into the open car window calmed and reassured Diana a little. A moon child was always reassured by the moon's presence.

Chapter XXXIV -
Licorice Root

Licorice root is known to aid heartburn and acid reflux, leaky gut, and adrenal fatigue. In addition, it is one of the main adaptogen herbs to lower cortisol. As a result, it helps immunity, coughs, sore throats, PMS, and menopause. It also relieves pain, regulates sebum production, and hydrates the skin.

In Spiritual Work: *Licorice is a root of love, fidelity, and commandment. Add licorice to a satchel with other commanding herbs and someone's name you wish to control. Drop the bag in the yard of their place of residence.*

John, the waiter, returned with the wine. Just in time to see the voyeurs watching as the cake box was delivered to the table across the room and started pouring for them to try.

"Ah, I was hoping to sing *Bonne Anniversaire*," Jean said, pepping up, not finding anything to be concerned about, referencing the French version of Happy Birthday, as he took his wine glass from Marco, tasted it, and nodded for him to proceed.

"Too strong, too soon," Shaka chastised as he took hold of his glass, "You know nothing about the woman. You have only been with one your whole life,"

"So, have you,"

"But I date,"

The women raised their glasses to them.

"You see," Jean commented, pleased with himself.

The gentlemen returned the gesture.

Shaka thought he could see a glow about her. It was the glow his mother had taught him to see in people's aura. One of the few skills he's sure she had learned from their secret Book, The Book he did not know of until it was too late. It had been some time since Shaka could see someone's aura so clearly. Shaka noticed he could see all of the women's auras as he looked. *How peculiar*, Shaka thought. His thoughts returned to his mother and aunt, to the conversation that made him become a historian.

'In time, the right people will come together, and our tribes will be reunited.' *whispered the memory of his mother's voice.*

Shaka couldn't help but feel optimistic, and his face reflected his wish. He hoped the right people looked like her. as the ladies got up from their table. The older of the two walked past them without saying a word. Surprisingly, the younger one walked over to them jovially, giving the men barely any time to stand up.

"Thanks for dinner," She smiled, kissing them both. "Sorry, they didn't come over. We're in a hurry."

"You're welcome," Jean called out as she left. Shaka laughed at the older man's face.

"I guess it was worth it," Shaka commented.

"*Cheri*, everything men do in life is done for women to smile at them. Did you see her ring?"

"No," Shaka answered. "Your eyes are still quick. What about it?"

"Nothing. It was interesting that a girl like that would be wearing a replica of one of Solomon's Seals."

"Really?"

"Really."

"Which one?"

"The pentagram, and no, it was not just a pentagram. It was a seal,"

"Interesting," Rubbing his hands together, Shaka jokes, "Maybe the magical women were keeping the room warmer. Now, it is almost frigid."

"Maybe it's just you, my friend," Jean replied, trying to sound nonchalant,

However, knowing that Shaka had the same abilities as his son and late wife. Jean wasn't sure if an unwanted presence hadn't entered the restaurant with them. The kind of presence that wasn't easily seen. But left only the coldness as an identifier for those with extrasensory abilities.

Whoever is here is not here for me, Jean thought. *I've already made my deal with the devils.* Still, he wanted to leave the restaurant as quickly as possible.

The waiter returned for their main orders, recommending the fish entree, which paired best with the wine they were drinking. Jean quickly agreed. Jean agreed the suggestion was perfect. As the men were exhausted, the entree would be ready faster.

Shaka wasn't ready to end the night and persuaded the older man to have a nightcap before leaving the restaurant. After dinner and over scotch, Shaka confessed to Jean that his mind was still on the woman. It had been nearly two decades since he had felt such a pull from someone. Jean was also fascinated with the group, wondering out loud why a young girl would have such a symbolic ring. Shaka was barely listening. Instead, his attention was on the empty table the group of women had left.

"I must be more tired than I thought," Shaka wondered, "or maybe it's the Scotch after the drive, but my vision seems to be acting up,"

"Oh," Jean remarketed, as a cold shiver passed at Shaka's word, "I guess it's time to go. We're not too far from home,"

The two men took less than 15 minutes to arrive at Jean's seven-bedroom, eight-bath, two-story, four-thousand-square-foot beachfront family home. The house was spectacular. Shaka had known Jean for a long time; however, this was the first time since Jean appeared in his classroom at the University of South Africa. Their time together had been like a whirlwind partnership of non-stop movement. Shaka was continuously learning new things about his benefactor. But, unquestionably, something like finally being invited to Jean's private residence meant they had reached another level in their friendship. They drove through large steel gates that swung slowly open, activated via an app on Jean's phone that he had fun showing Shaka.

They walked through the ten-foot-tall doors designed with rose vines made of iron overlaid on the thick glass. Shaka expected to find the hauntings of an old French mansion as he had seen in the movies, with dark drapes covering the custom fleur-de-lis wallpapers, a large number of statues standing guard over deep-cushioned, flower-covered antique furniture, and an air, stale from lack of circulation.

However, when the lights came on, Shaka was pleasantly surprised by Jean's home. The house was very modern, with an open floor plan. The off-white walls held paintings of landscapes. The wall directly across from the men was a two-story high. Wholly made of glass that looked out to the beach. It was divided by a white ornamented wrought-iron balcony. On the first floor, light-colored furniture was arranged tastefully. One room flowed into the next, unobstructed.

"Let me give you a tour so you don't get lost,"

Jean quickly showed him the first floor, the dining room, living room, and chef's kitchen, before escorting him to the elevator with his bag.

"I want to be you when I grow up," Shaka whistled, his overnight bag in hand.

"No, you don't. Ownership of empty homes does not make up for a lonely heart. If I had to do it over again, I would have chosen Esperanza's life above all of it."

On the second floor, as they exited the elevator, Jean gave Shaka a quick tour of the library, whose shelves were heavily lined with antique books from authors who died centuries ago. There was an antique Chippendale desk; the old man stood there for a minute, leisurely tracing the bureau's top with his fingertips, as Shaka watched quietly.

"She would sit here for hours with Mateo on her lap,"

Shaka felt sad for him. He did not know what it was to lose a love like that. In thirty-five years, Shaka had never remarried. He'd had some good relationships, but ultimately, his soul told him they were incorrect.

Iye, his mother, told him he should always trust his gut. Yet, in moments like this, with Jean so vulnerable, he didn't understand why sometimes warning bells went off about Jean.

"Come, I'll show you to your room," Jean continued, leading them past the elevator.

"Even all the money in the world can't fight a disease like cancer. I'm sure Esperanza was happy and knew how much you loved her,"

"*Oui*, cancer," Jean responded quietly.

Shaka followed the old man down the hall when he stopped and put his bag down to look at the ocean.

"Jean," The older man stopped. "How long have you owned this house?"

"I don't know, maybe thirty years. Why?"

"Have you ever stopped to enjoy this view?" Shaka asked reflectively while staring out at the full moon over the ocean.

"We had the whole back wall reinforced Category 5 hurricane windproof glass, just to enjoy Mother Nature's splendor," Jean sighed, "But truthfully, my friend, I was always so busy, I didn't take the time to enjoy it,"

He looked up for the first time since Jean walked into the house. He smiled at the younger man beside him and looked out into the abyss. The moon was heavy with a yellowish tint, making the old man in the white suit look luminescent. Only a few stars could be seen in the sky over the dark waters.

"Not as often as I should have, my friend, not as often as I should." After a pause, he continued. "The most beautiful gift of nature is that it gives one pleasure to look around and try to comprehend what one sees."

"Einstein?"

"*Oui.*"

As Shaka continued to look out the window, he thought he saw a faint etching in the glass. He moved closer and squinted to have a better look. It looked like an exotic artist's imaginative creation on the glass, with a few pentagrams, hexagrams, and other shapes scattered around. Finally, Jean saw where his attention was. A six-pointed star inside of a circle.

Inside each gap of the star was a different symbol in Hebrew. Shaka ran his fingers across the glass. Some constellations and prayers were written in dead languages that no one was likely to decipher.

"Ah, the protective seal. You will find crystals, seals, and other things that interest you in this house. Unfortunately, I made a lot of money from many things and did not take the time to understand the consequences beforehand. The older she got, the more vulnerable I felt, and the deeper I dove into the occult mysteries. Soon, I worried about what I might have unintentionally exposed Esperanza to. We might not have Esperanza's Book to protect us much longer, but besides The Book being protective, we knew very little about it since she hadn't had a chance to learn more before it came into our possession. Jean sighed. "Most of the books in the library are reprints of the originals. We could not keep them safe here this close to the ocean."

"I was going to ask about that," Shaka confessed, picking up his bag and seeming relieved. They were about to walk away when a spark of light caught their attention. "Hey, what's that over there?"

Both men strained to see down the beach.

"That looks like miles down the coast. Probably at another residency, over the bridge." Jean shrugged, continuing to walk down the hall.

Shaka looked at his watch. It was only 11:35 p.m. *So close to the witching hour,* he thought. "Well, they have the right idea for a full moon night."

"I guess," Jean remarked solemnly, "I'll put you in one of Mateo's guest rooms. They all have a television," Jean responded as if that was a suitable replacement for the bonfire. Shaka moaned behind the older man.

"There's also a reprint of the first edition copy of *"Egypt: The Cradle of Masonry"* in there that will put you right to sleep." Both men laughed, walking on.

On the parts of the hallway walls were paintings by Renaissance artists that Shaka was unfamiliar with. The images were hung in golden frames against the white paint. Finally, they reached a large, dark wooden door, and Jean swung it open, reaching across the inner wall to flip on the light.

This is a guest room, Shaka thought. He could put his living room and kitchen into this single bedroom.

In the center was a mahogany brown four-poster bed well made with a tan comforter set. The posters had parallel striations that ran down their length and had a pinecone design on the tops. Across the bed was a nine-drawer dresser made of the same wood, with a large flat-screen TV. And in the corner was a stocked bookshelf.

Jean remained outside as Shaka walked in. Placing his bag on the bed, he felt an overwhelming urge to stretch.

"God, I didn't realize how tight I was from the ride down. I guess I'm more tired than I thought. But at least my vision is better," Shaka admitted, walking toward a closed door he thought might be the bathroom.

"Seems like we both are not as young as we used to be." Jean yawned. "I'm glad you are here, Shaka. I hope you know I appreciate our friendship. Good night."

Shaka barely heard the old man inside the large bathroom with a sunken clawfoot tub. But before Shaka could reply, Jean had closed the door behind him and left.

****

Too quickly, the brothers were reminded that nothing was ever simple throughout their history with this project. They hadn't expected to find Jean having dinner at a restaurant. Much less, accompanied by Shaka Solomon. Or to be seated behind a group of women giving off such intense magical energy, interacting with Jean and Shaka.

The brothers were already ill-prepared to have Shaka there. The coven of what had to be black witches was powerful. The eldest watched them, keeping the twins cloaked from the whole restaurant. This drained Ahkter to the point of exhaustion. He barely reached his sit to collapse in it. Feebly Ahkter wondered if this restaurant was some kind of safe space for their type. As the nearby Oak Room was for The Sons of Eve.

After a while, the twins' alarm turned into frustration. When they realized that Philia was not joining her uncle. Lacking the energy it would take for the pair to move without being seen. The twins waited for the women to leave, then Jean and Shaka before slinking back into their rental car and heading for the hotel room they had requisitioned.

Chapter XXXV – *Sorrel*

Sorrel is exceptionally high in vitamin C, a water-soluble vitamin that fights inflammation and plays a crucial role in immune function. It's also high in fiber, promoting regularity, increasing feelings of fullness, and helping stabilize blood sugar levels.

In Spiritual Work: *Carry to protect against heart disease. Place in sickrooms to aid in recuperation from illnesses and wounds.*

'Everything will work out as it's supposed to,' the other voice in her head affirmed.

As they were getting out of the Wrangler. The three women stopped to watch as Gerda and Leatrice got out, dressed in white. Gerda was a petite woman with deep brown eyes, an easy, caring smile, and golden skin. Leatrice had a gift in her hand as she walked straight up to Ceres. Her shiny chrome glasses reflected the streetlamp. Leatrice's hair was now dyed red where previously it had been brown, but besides that, the professor looked precisely the same as when she'd taken her class.

"Sorry, we're late," Diana offered.

"It's okay," Gerda smiled, "we're the ones crashing the party,"

"Happy birthday, Ms. Bastille. And thank you for inviting us. I'm so sorry to be crashing your party at the last minute," Leatrice smiled as she kissed Ceres. "I didn't know how young you were when you were in my class. Wow, I am about to graduate Pre-Med and just turned twenty-two. That is truly black girl magic."

Magalie burst out laughing at how ironic this statement was.

"Sorry," the youngest member of the group apologized, regaining her composure. "I'm going to go put the cake on the counter."

"Thank you, but it wasn't magic," Ceres smiled, but there was a dull ringing in her head,

"Just a Haitian mother that always expects the best from us."

"And maybe a little magic," Diana responded, winking at Gerda as she walked into the house.

Gerda laughed and shook her head, making her now-graying mane of hair bounce in the moonlight. The wink was a reminder of a moderate bit of magic Diana and Gerda had done to try to save Gerda's husband once upon a time.

Gerda was always in awe of Di. They were only two years apart in age, with Gerda being the senior, but they were worlds apart when it came to areas of knowledge. Gerda had been raised in a strict Haitian household that followed the three cardinal rules for raising girls: *l'eglise, lacaye, and l'ecole*. The only things a proper girl needed to be a good mother, wife, and servant to her community were the church, home, and school. Over the years, Gerda had learned as much as she felt comfortable knowing without feeling like she was betraying her faith. Even though the line between beckoning the Spirit of Vodou for aid and favor. Or petitioning, the Church's saints were very thin, if not utterly merged, in some parts of their homeland. But Diana, on the other hand, believed in the many paths to God and that we limited ourselves by limiting the ways we connect to Her.

Gerda watched something keep pulling her child to a more Spiritual path as the years progressed. In the end, Leatrice stayed in the church with her mother. When Charles became ill, Western medicine and prayer weren't working. Diana's herbs and teachings on energy healing and sharing had given Gerda and her husband more time than the doctors could. Gerda learned there is always an even trade, life for life, when you ask the universe for anything.

They could have traded life force if it had been more than just the two. Ultimately, the women had been okay with sacrificing a few chickens, a small goat, and a thirty-pound pig, which they feasted on. But each sacrifice brought less and less time to his life. Ultimately, Gerda and Diana weren't willing to go far enough to extend his life by more than a few years. But Gerda was still very grateful for the time they'd given him. Since then, Gerda has found a happy medium between her faith and Spirituality. But unfortunately, that balance was about to be thrown straight off the boat.

The women walked through the home's front door, the light of the moon cascading through the double sliding glass doors of the living room overlooking the crashing seas. The off-white furniture seemed to glow, and the hanging plants looked like shadowy figures waiting to approach. Gerda sighed at the scene;

she loved this house. Magalie walked in after them, turning on the lights as she placed the cake safely on a table before walking out the back door. There were only a few minutes before the clock would strike midnight, solidifying Ceres' twenty-second birthday. Then, it was time to get the fire outside started.

Ceres came strolling in last and breathing deeply as the ringing in her ears intensified. She turned around to look outside at the moon door before locking it, and its glare hurt her eyes. The knots in her stomach were now feeling uncontrollable.

Inside the house, Diana prepared a silver tray with herbs, wine, and spices as offerings to the voodoo Spirits while she directed Gerda, who was in the pantry, to get more wine. It was Leatrice's first time in the house, and she was in love from her initial step into the doorway. Gerda knew the feeling; it was a fantastic house. But more than that, it was a loving house. The house had a way of comforting its guests from the moment they walked in until they left, no matter what room they found themselves in. The vaulted ceiling and free-flowing ocean wind encouraged guests to breathe more deeply of life. And the floor-to-ceiling glass back wall made their eyes dilate, enlarging their vision.

Ceres barely smiled at the look on her professor's face when she came through the front door.

"Hey, Batman!" the professor smiled, pleasantly surprised to find a Batman throw cover on the couch.

"Feel free to look around. I have to get something from upstairs," Ceres advised, cutting through the kitchen quickly. A sense that she had to get to The Book overcame her.

As Ceres approached the flower wallpaper hall entrance, a bluish glow from her bedroom slowed her steps. Cautiously, she continued down the hall, not bothering to turn on the light. Moving forward, a little out of curiosity and a little out of compulsion. A part of Ceres was not completely surprised to find this light. It was familiar to her, an unknown known. And the closer she moved towards her bedroom door, the more inviting the light became.

But why here, now, she wondered.

Ceres stepped forward into her open bedroom door. The intensity of the glow emerging from it blinded her. Forced her to squint as she tried to move forward and pinpoint the source of it. With her hands extending in front of her, Ceres moved slowly forward.

Downstairs in the living, Diana rushed to get things prepared. She felt the time change before she saw the alarm on her phone. Officially signifying her daughter's 22nd birthday, as she suddenly lost consciousness from the abrupt loss of energy.

"Shit," She swore, coming in a second later, putting down the tray, and heading for her daughter's bedroom.

"You, okay?" Gerda called after her.

"Hurry with the stones,"

Ceres hit her chin on the edge of the bed frame upstairs with a thud.

"Fuck!" she shouted louder than usual, her eyes reflexively squeezing shut from the pain. A moment later, when she opened them up again, the world around her was gone.

Her winged friend was sitting in the lotus position, reading The Book on what appeared to be a hazy replica of her bed in a featureless, utterly white room. He looked up quizzically as he acknowledged her. Then, one second later, the bed was gone, and Tellus held The Book open before her. The outline of his gossamer thread form was only identifiable by her subconscious. The large brown Book seemed to be the only substance left behind.

'Now, you will see,'

"Now, I will see," Ceres confirmed monotonically.

Ceres felt like the words were coming through her. As well as from the numerous other women connected to her. The text rose from the pages like golden dust, taking shape in the air before her. Each echoed in her mind before she spoke it.

"*Comme ci-dessus donc ci-dessous*. As above, so below, I call upon that most Ineffable holy Name of God, IAH, and pray, bestow onto me wisdom; Divine and terrestrial, bind my Spirit so I may always look upon you even with open eyes, and unbind my flesh, so I may never succumb to earthly domination, in the essence of The First Woman."

'*And so, it shall be*,' Tellus confirmed with a bow,

His form dissipated into a vapor of glowing light particles, which flowed into Ceres' opened mouth and nose. The young woman rose to the tip of her toes, filled with divine light. It entered her and surrounded her until it finally engulfed her. It was the deafening sound of someone foolish enough to stand inside a bell when it struck twelve. Her body vibrated from within, the invisible sound coursing through her, shaking her apart, deconstructing her until she became nothingness.

The vibration rippled from Ceres and reverberated through the house, draining a part of the energy of anyone inside. Causing Gerda to lose her breath for a second and further weaken Diana.

The young Priestess stood there unmoving. Her toes barely supported her form as the hidden history of the world played like a three-dimensional, virtual reality experience behind her closed eyes.

***

Outside, Magalie and Leatrice hadn't taken long to start the bonfire in the Bastilles' regular spot. Diana had installed a 3-ft round silver fire pit about 40 feet from their house. The hole was bracketed by large white boulders for guests to sit on and had been one of her first additions to the home. To the east, the bracket opened onto the water. While in the West, a large flat stone sat to position offerings to throw into fire. Or for the current storytellers to sit on, which Diana insisted. Or a place to put the cooler on and off the hot sand, which Magalie emphasized.

Leatrice was sitting in the half-circle with the flames from the firewood dancing in the air. She listened to the wood cracking against the crashing waves while watching Magalie. Magalie seemed restless. She kept getting up just to sit right back down. Leatrice and Magalie waited for the rest of the women to join them under the full moon night.

"You, okay?" Leatrice finally asked.

"Fine, just..., I'm not sure. Something," Magalie advised, rolling her shoulders and stretching as she sat back down next to Leatrice once more, pulling up the hood of her sweater.

"Yeah, it feels like something different is in the air," Leatrice confirmed.

Magalie's anxiety seemed to have peaked as she stood again. Then, from the corner of her eyes, Magalie saw something approaching that was brighter than the flames in front of them.

Magalie turned entirely around and saw the figure of her sister inside the glow. She was instantly reminded of that story. The Ceres that had gone upstairs to retrieve The Book was gone. Through the flames, Magalie could sense her sister was not in control. Inside the house, Diana felt it too — even from the floor, even barely conscious. It moved through the walls like a tide coming in. She had felt something like it once before, decades ago, the night Ceres was born and the midwife had gone quiet in a way that was not alarm but awe. Diana had not understood it then. She understood it now. Her daughter had arrived.

To be continued

Good Food

An Understanding Of Basic Alchemy

The Daughters of Lilith Series

BOOK 3

Luna Charles

About the author

Luna Charles, is a Haitian-American writer who has authored numerous books, articles, and essays. Besides being an accomplished author, Luna is also a dedicated student of Theology, Metaphysics, and Philosophy. As a mother of two lovely girls, Luna has spent most of her life in South Florida.